A GUIDE TO READING

©Paul Gallantry, 2004, 2011
ISBN: 978-1-4476-8020-8

A fool sees not the same tree that a wise man sees.

One

In a series of increasingly irritating interludes to the narrative, the author introduces himself and comments upon his incipient creation, along with observations of a trivial and foolish kind.

I believe it was Pasteur who said something along the lines of 'Chance favours the well-prepared mind'. Well, in that case, I can expect no great opportunity to befall me, as I am utterly unprepared for the task ahead of me. A whole story in a single day! What a stupid enterprise to enter without a notion in the head as to plot, characterisation, and whatnot. Yet, I am determined to give it a shot. I am, as you may guess, the author of the following sad story, in which – what? The plot is, so far, nonexistent, the characters a series of mere wisps of the imagination, the scenes in which all shall be played out nothing but speculation. As such, there is clearly a need to, as it were, pad things out a bit, with a digressionary chapter here and an aside there, or the judicious (or not) use of quotes and summaries to head my chapters. Besides, I see no reason why I may not intrude upon the action as I see fit, as and when I want, just as Henry Fielding did in Tom Jones. This is my piece of fiction and I may do with it as I will, and hang the consequences. The consequence, of course, being that no-one is likely to read this (save my aged, future self, cackling over it), but, well, this is meant to be a bit of amusement. Of course, if you're one of those readers who just wants to get on with the action, you can quite easily avoid these rambles altogether; I feel, however, that you may be missing out – after all, the rambling road is all the more interesting than the motorway.

So here, I present my tale. At the moment, it involves a man in a pub. I don't know what's going to happen next; At the moment, he is just sitting there, nursing a pint at around half past one in the afternoon, wondering what to do next. The location: My home village, in my hometown, namely Emmer Green, in Reading, Berkshire. After all, one of the exhortations to any new novelist is to write about what one knows, and why not start with the pub I know best in the world? And the character's name? Let us call him Dan. And why write about Reading, of all places? Well, as I said, because I know it; But also, because no-one else ever has written much regarding the place, as far as I'm aware; Hardy calls it Aldbrickham, and is not particularly nice about it; Jerome K. Jerome denigrates it; Defoe praises its wealth; and that's about it. Of course, the Reading I write about should not be confused with Reading, the real place, just as one should not confuse a fictional character with someone who ostensibly resembles him or her, even though they share the same name, family, clothes, opinions, lovers and so forth. No, the town is as much a character as Dan, even if it is a boring one. This is Reading as a metaphysical place, and yes, I am well aware I can here spluttered laughter erupting from the mouths of any reader who lives in it, or who has had the pleasure of getting lost on its ring road. It is metaphysical inasmuch as any real place can be made representative of other things. It must be said that Reading is about as solid and real a place as you could hope to visit; For that reason, let us try to render it as evanescent as cloud, and the characters that appear in it as solid as the bricks from which the physical place is built.

As the author of this tale, I'm not sure what's going to happen next; I am as swept along with all this as you are, so permit me to be not so much the Chorus to this story, as an interested bystander, drifting behind my own creation, recording his every move along the way, using different voices to catch him. That is, of course, if he deigns to move – I'm not sure how much he likes his pint, or lounging in this pub on a sunny afternoon in July, smoke furling in the light from languid cigarettes and an international football match on the TV in the corner. I feel, however, there is some frustration building within him, and that some other shall come along presently. Now, of course, the problem arises: How to present him?

Which narrative style to use? Externally? Let my voice alone guide, present, manipulate and swoop through each character as and when? Perhaps different perspectives: the character seen through the lens of a camera, a layer of smoky fug, a police report, a diary entry, someone's email, a hastily scribbled note, a lover's letter, a court summons, a news report. It will immediately be obvious that our hero, and all those others who may appear, will appear to be almost completely different people according to which perspective I, the author, use. The only way of being certain of whom is being described is from a physical perspective, and that is itself unreliable: I don't even know what my character looks like yet. So, how about internal monologues? We gain a perspective on the individual's psyche, but it is a necessarily limited perspective, a view restricted by what the teller of the tale can know, see and feel – and again, it makes our story tenuous. Well then, and how else? Photography? Cartoons? This is an exercise in words, not pictures, so that counts those out. Dialogue solely? Perhaps. Descriptions of coughs, shuffles, movements of hands, gestures, looks? Maybe. Crosswords, acrostics, logic puzzles? Entertaining, possibly.

Merely by writing, as I write, possibilities start queuing up to be counted and used – the whys and wherefores of those phantoms, my characters, rising to feed on the blood of the pen and utter what they must; Different possibilities for writing styles and perspectives parade for my inspection; And the reader – the great Objective Reader, for whom I write – who are you? What would you like to read? How shall I entertain you? Your host I must be; Here is the scene, here the bill of fare; I hope you will be amused and fed, and then go on your way content. And so, let us swing into the scene, and find, for want of a better word, the hero of this book. There he is; His back is to us as we come in the door; In his mid-thirties, although he looks younger, except for the streaks of grey in his hair, which has just begun to thin; Handsome, but haunted, and his face is scowling into his pint; a lit cigarette is in his left hand, and his right holds a pen, and he is scrawling over a crossword. He is arranging some letters in a circle, and then reading them backwards and forwards, side to side, up and down. His circling pen stops, then rapidly he writes seven letters in one of the clues. It says:

Two: At the sign of the White Horse
Turning and turning in the widening gyre, the falcon cannot hear the falconer.

W.B.Yeats

In which our hero, Dan Thompson, ponders his thunderingly tedious life, and seeks escape; Upon which he meets an unexpected friend from the past; They have a drink, then the friend suggests moving on to another bar.

'FUCK OFF'.
'I'm sorry?'
'That's what I've just written. Fuck off. Begone. Go away, you fucking weirdo, and stop staring at me like that'
'Oh..sorry...'
And off he fucked, the weirdo. He looked like a scarecrow, with unkempt hair, staring blue eyes, unshaven and overweight.
I was at the end of my tether. I felt knackered, lost and unwanted. Here I was, thirty-five, and hideously aware of time's rapidly spinning thread. I was pondering what I'd managed to do up till then with my life, and I didn't really like any of the answers coming back my way. Sure, I'd been abroad for most of the past decade and had had a blast, but it had been a voluntary exile in many ways: When I'd left, the country had been a total shithole, as was my life. Now, I was back, and here I still was, in my old boozer, with the same faces lining the bar as from before, living the same lives, and me back as though nothing had changed at all. I felt bilious and weary. It seemed to me that my foreign sojourns had been nothing more than an escape, an adventure, a diversion from the dour realities of Reading. What I found even more galling is that they hadn't had the good sense to leave off decorating the White Horse. Where it used to be liberally caked in crappy old prints, horse brasses, dodgy plates and strange fire implements, and stink of rancid grease, cigarettes and urinals, it was now a place where you would happily bring children. Outside, it had decking, complete with large sun umbrellas and heaters. It was open plan. It had Sky TV, which was at this point in my tale churning out some international friendly. It had a non-smoking dining area. It even

had an aquarium. Actually, the latter wasn't too bad; When the talk became tedious, I'd have something entertaining to stare at. And here I was, at half past one on a Friday afternoon in July, drinking beer and failing to do the sodding Araucaria crossword in the Guardian (as ever), and wondering what the Hell I should be doing with life. It was a hot day, and it was one of those that seems to simmer with frustration and regret. I had just walked out of a temporary job, had a damp room in a damp house with a couple of damp housemates who worked for a call centre, and I felt like I was going nowhere. Hell, I'd been debating with myself since 8 in the morning whether to go into town and check out the temporary job situation, or write off for some work abroad, or just go and do something different, but no, I ended up back in the good old White Horse again.

I knocked back my drink, then headed to the bar. The fucking weirdo was still there, nursing a pint of bitter and jotting something in a notebook, and occasionally muttering a word or giggling to himself. He glanced up at me, then put his nose back in his notebook and began scrawling frantically.
'A pint of Bass again', I said, and the barmaid (barMAID? She was at least fifty, with great sagging bingo wings flopping over red elbows, and a face like an overweight trout) filled up my glass. I looked at myself in the mirror, and behind me, at the seven or eight people ranged on sofas and barstools who were watching the match. Their faces were intent and fixed – the same kind of expressions you see whenever someone watches a not particularly interesting stretch of a game, or a play, or a debate, waiting to see the outcome of the next move. Myself, I looked weary, frustrated and beaten. I paid for the beer, then slunk off to my seat in the corner. I lit a fag, started trying to do the crossword again. Nothing. I flung my pen down again, and beat around in my own head for something, anything to do. Oh God, I muttered to myself. I've got to get my life together! For Christ's Sake get me something to do!

Now here's the laugh: Just as I'd thought that, the door opened. Call it divine intervention or diabolic or just an awful bit of literary plot-twisting (and why shouldn't life be like a bad book plot, anyway? Let's face it, most lives are twisted, confused, fearful and full of coincidences), but in walked someone I hadn't seen for almost four years: Taylor Coleridge.

Taylor and I had travelled together for nearly a year, working our way up from India, round the Arabian Peninsula, then through the Red Sea and Suez Canal and finally to Beirut, where I lost him in a bar. He was a brilliant companion to have on any journey: witty, conversational, knowledgeable, creative and prone to following his own whims. I don't think he'd ever settled down anywhere, but preferred to wander, merely because he could. In a way, he was somewhat like his near-namesake, Samuel Taylor Coleridge, but without the laudanum or pomposity. After losing him, I'd continued up around the Mediterranean coast, while he, as I learnt from other people and from one badly torn letter and a few brief emails from him, had headed back into the desert, then up onto the Silk Road and subsequently towards China. While I would expect to find him in an Algerian souk, a Turkish pazar, on a camel in Tajikistan or on the summit of a mountain I'd just climbed, one place I'd never expect him was here on my home turf.

He saw me and smiled his lazy, feline smile.
'Ah, there you are', he said.
After I'd gawped for too long to look anything other than a bit dumb, I said.
'Jesus! Long time no see, my man! How are you!'
'Same as ever. Just chilling, thought I'd come along and see how you are. Nice place, this. How are you?'
'Ah, you know, not bad, not bad. The same. What are you drinking?'

I got us a beer and we sat down together. I asked him a few things about his travels and what he'd been up to, and he sketched them in for me. He seemed to be a bit more taciturn and less upbeat than I'd have expected, but then again it had been almost four years since we last met.

'So what happened to you last time we were together? I got up for a slash, I come back, you've buggered off.'

'I could say the same for you, Dan. I lean over to chat with that most enchanting babe, I turn around, and you were no longer there. I looked around, I couldn't find you, someone said, there's a party round the corner, do you want to come, I went, you were left behind. That's the way it was.'
'You could have tried to find me.'
'You could have done the same.'
'True. Sorry.'
'Nothing to be sorry for. Here we both are, on this fine July day, drinking beer in your local in your home town…what could be better?'
'Yeah.'

We drank our pints in silence for a while and watched the TV.

'She says hello, by the way.'
'Who?'
'You know. Beattie.'
I was stunned briefly. Beattie was….well, Beattie. I'd been pretty intense with her a couple of years previously, although when it came down to it, circumstances had conspired in such a way that we never really got it together, and in fact, I'd been thinking about her that morning, wondering about What Ifs.
'How the hell do you know her?'
'You talked about her often enough – and I saw photos of you two together. Anyway, I came across her in Bangkok. Recognised her straight away, said hello, mentioned your name. This was two weeks ago.'
'Jesus! Really? How was she?'
'She was good, very fine –and, in fact, thinking about you. She's kind of the reason I'm here. I was heading for the UK and she still had your address. I decided to check it out, thinking to have a beer on the way, and here we are.'
'So what was she up to?'
'Still teaching- still single. My man, you must have really done something to her – when I told her I was heading back this way, she asked me to look you up. Said she had some kind of premonition that you needed help, something like that, and your last email had sounded like someone in jail. And looking at you, I'd say she's about right.'

'What's that meant to mean?'
'I mean you look miserable as sin.'
He looked straight at me, and he was absolutely right. I was miserable. What could I say? I lit another cigarette.
'Ah, shit, Taylor, I don't know. You're spot on, but I don't know what to do. I'm stuck here and I can't see a way forward, it's like, well, I don't know, like I'm in the middle of a big wood in the middle of the night and I can't see a way out. I feel – well, I feel lost, I guess.'
'That's not like you.'
'It's this place. It's England. Once I got back here, it was as if all the travelling and working in all those places hadn't happened, like some kind of dream. No-one was interested, no-one wanted to know –you know, 'so what was it like?', and you start, and they go 'hm, yes''.
And I spilled it out – the months of frustration, the shitty jobs in anonymous offices, the whole hateful trudge of the nine-to-five with a whole bunch of others who hated their jobs, their lives and each other, and above all, man's total indifference unto man. Taylor listened quietly, and bought another round.
'So why don't you get out again?'
A good question, but how could I answer? I was stuck; that was the only answer I could give. The sunlight edged round the carpet; the match on the TV came to an end; and it came towards three.
Taylor knocked back his pint.
'Come on, finish off,' he ordered.
'Why? Where we off to?'
'To find yourself again, Dan T. To find yourself again. Beattie was right, you need rescuing. This is what we'll do; let's saunter into town, wander from place to place, and try to find where your soul went, my man.'
'Does this involve getting thoroughly drunk?!?'
'That's the idea.'
Well, what else was there to do, but neck my pint, have a slash, then follow Taylor Coleridge as he led me down towards the wild hub of Reading on a Friday afternoon, evening and night?
As we came out of the pub, the weirdo I'd seen before sidled past us, glanced at me again, coughed an apology and crept around the corner. Suddenly, it felt good to be in sunlight again,

especially with my old friend and the prospect of doing something rather than fester by myself. I felt a current of excitement, as if I was back to my journeys once more.
'Shall we take the bus?'
'No, we'll have to wait ages from here. Let's walk down the hill and catch one in Caversham.'
As we walked past the duck pond and down Peppard road, I noticed that someone had somehow managed to uproot, haul and then dump the sign that said 'WELCOME TO READING. TWINNED WITH DUSSELDORF' from Henley Road and lay it on the strip of grass by the bus shelter, which had, as ever, been kicked in and graffitti'd by some arsehole. The word HELL, in large red letters, was sprayed on it.
'Nice welcome', said Taylor.
We carried on walking down the road, past Buckingham Drive and Sheepwalk, where we could see the town beneath us, drowsy in a reddish haze; The gasometers at the confluence of the Thames and Kennet, the shopping centres squatting in the town, the church spires pointing upwards feebly between the tower blocks. We hit Caversham, and stopped in the Prince of Wales for a quick one. Sitting on the patio, we watched a large group of teenagers, all of them riddled with acne and all looking sullen and hateful in a way that only an English teenager can, wander past, then stop and go back, then redouble their steps once more. They were arguing between themselves about where to go, what to do. One argued for sitting on the bench on Balmore hill, another said to sit on a bench in the park, while someone else suggested sitting by the river. They went first this way, then another, aimless, pestered by flies or wasps, which hovered round the alcopops they had clutched in their hands Fuckwits.

Three: How do you read?

One glance at a book and you hear the voice of another person, perhaps someone dead for 1,000 years. To read is to voyage through time.

　　　　　　　　　　　　　　　　　　　　Carl Sagan

In which the Author returns to pontificate; He comments upon the action and characters so far, hopefully pre-empting bilious comments from the critical reader.

You choose a book; One from your own personal library perhaps, something you haven't read before, or a tattered, dog-eared old friend that you haven't seen for a while and wish to become reacquainted with. Or your local friendly librarian hands over a hardback title, one covered in a battered plastic wrap, that smells of mustiness and many hands, and contains tatters of past lives as bookmarks: a bus ticket, a torn piece of note, a used cotton bud, complete with waxy residue. Or you're at the airport and you hurriedly buy something chunky with a glossy cover, where the author's name is written large and the title, which contains the definite article and a word like 'protocol' or 'dossier', is written small, and you hope it will suffice for the beach – junk food novelry. Or you find, cleaning out an old cupboard, all those books you once had to read at school, and all the ones that you never had time for, and you pick out one in wonder, then blow off the dust.

And then you open the book. You glance at the first page, with the title, the author's name and the publisher. What do you do then? How do you read? In this world, there are so many things to read, and so many things from which a meaning can be inferred if 'read' in the correct way. Long, long ago, long before our ancestors invented pictograms and hieroglyphs and abstract symbols that conveyed a sound or a meaning, they could read the sky, the wind, the movement of animals, the flash of a red eye in the dark, the meaning of a face. Back then, mystery and understanding were one, as simple as times when fog rolls over land and makes the solid earth and ephemeral, changing air into one thing. The painting of animals on cave walls rendered them real – if you looked at the painting for long enough, you would find yourself watching a herd of the real thing, and if you were watching a herd of bison, then pretty soon you would find yourself in the depths of a cavern, looking up at a painting composed of a few lines. But then along came symbols and hieroglyphs and writing, and suddenly what we see as 'real' and what we see as 'mystery' were pulled asunder. The more that was written, the more that various meanings were piled upon even the most innocent word, so that to extrapolate the true meaning of any given sound or symbol required extravagant lengths of interpretation. This infection of the written word spread in time to the uttered word, so now when someone says 'hello', it can be interpreted in many ways: Is the speaker sincere, is it a genuine greeting, is he angry with me, and so forth. And as writing spread, so there were more things to read, and the more there was to read, the ways to read things became many and varied. Look at this list of things: A label in a skirt; A cigarette packet; A bus ticket; A newspaper front page; A newspaper article on the economy; A religious book; A comic; A novel by a respected, 'serious' writer; A novel by a populist writer; a cookery book; A poster for a concert; a text message; a job advert; the telephone directory.

Now tell me, do you read all these in the same way? What would happen if you did?

Of course we don't, because then all these things would either be imbued with tremendous significance or none at all. Then again, perhaps everything is significant; Perhaps everything we read has layer upon layer of meaning. That's the problem with words – what may seem the simplest phrase can suddenly elude the grasp of even the best-read of us. And then there is the simple matter of reading a book. Some people, after leafing through the first chapter, will then skip to the very last page to see the outcome. These characters are the type of person who wants to know what's ahead of them at all times, in order to render their lives simple. Then there are those who read a classic, then read the introduction (usually by some academic) afterwards; They are people who wish to have the book's secrets unlocked for them and their ideas confirmed. And what about the type of reader who races through page after page, wolfing down great gobbets of a writer's delicately crafted fare, merely in order to reach the end and claim to have read it? Don't invite this character to a gourmet meal: they'll tear it limb from limb, then belch loudly and go to the nearest McDonald's. There is the languid dipper, who picks at a chapter here and there, never deigning to do anything so gauche as to actually finish a book from start to end.

But then there is that rarest of readers, the participant in the text. He or she reads diligently, carefully, with neither too much attention to significance, nor too little, who treasures a writer's craft without coddling it. This reader will carefully consider what the author has proffered, tasting it thoroughly and accepting or rejecting as necessary. It is far too easy to be precious about books, but the truth is that a story has to be tough, considering the battering it will get at the hands of the reader and the critic.

What I am trying to say, I suppose, is please be gentle with this tale! I can only do my best; and if so far you have not enjoyed the tale, what can I do? I'm as stuck right now as you are. However, you are in the fortunate position of being able to skip a few pages, or right to the end, or pick languidly if you wish, while we poor creatures must trudge through line after line to ascertain our fate. A reader, in truth, can travel in time through the individual universe that each tale proffers – you can see the characters' future fates, then flick back and watch as we reach it. Even if you don't like what you've seen so far, bear with me – it's going to start getting interesting in the next chapter. Well, I hope so..

You may have surmised that I, the Author, am a fictional construct. Indeed, you may have seen how I seem to have been fitted into the tale. You may be right, you may not be. If it is the case that I'm fictional, why has my written style changed? The first few paragraphs of this interlude do not much resemble those of the first chapter; so what is happening?

There are two possibilities:

Either I am an appalling writer, and cannot create a consistent style, or:

I am taking the piss somewhat.

Whichever way you guess, you can't be certain.

Can you see me grinning?

But what to say of Dan Thompson and Taylor Coleridge thus far? The latter, I'm sure you will agree, has an absolutely ridiculous, but strangely rather cool, name. Now, let's not pretend this is, in any way, shape or form, a non-fiction tale; therefore both Dan and Taylor are ciphers for something else, even if the former has expressed himself with all too real emotion. How we read the characters and their situation will inform how we see their tale, even if we read more into it than is intended. So, we have someone in a pub, having a drink and feeling depressed; An old friend of his walks in and mentions his lover; they finish their drinks and start walking towards town, stopping off for a small drink on the way, which is where they are frozen for the moment. It might be salutary, at this point, to keep tabs on how much they have drunk; After all, this might be fiction, but we don't want to ruin it by having them drink life-threatening quantities of alcohol and still function like real people. So far, then, Dan has had three pints of Bass and a bottle of lager in the Prince of Wales; Taylor has had two pints of lager and a bottle of same. Since we joined the tale at two o'clock, we can presume, I think, that Dan has had something to eat. This will keep him on his feet for the next few hours. I have a feeling that the pair of them are going to consume considerably more in the next few hours. Then again, have you considered the possibility that Taylor Coleridge is no more than a figment of Dan's depressed imagination? I know, it's the old 'And suddenly I woke up and it had all been a dream' scenario; Perhaps it is, perhaps it isn't; Shall we go and find out?

Four: across the Dark River and into the Maelstrom

It was the best of times, it was the worst of times…..
                                          Charles Dickens
In which our heroes cross the Thames by Reading Bridge; They reach the Blagrave pub and there encounter some great thinkers; And past the Town hall come face to face with a stag party and a hen party.

'Come on, there's a bus, let's grab it!'
We needn't have hurried; there was a large queue waiting at the bus stop in front of the playing fields in Westfield road. For such a warm and sunny day, this group seemed a miserable bunch. There were a few pensioners shuffling forwards and a pair of harassed-looking mothers with young kids, who all seemed to be having an unhappy time of it..
' I'm late as it is!' shouted the bus driver. 'Come on love, on you get, I haven't got all day…that's it, on you get, put it over there….can I see your pass, lovely…there you are…'
He punched out tickets and checked passes as people fed coins into the machine. One kid, about eighteen months old, was bawling its eyes out.
'Hello there', he grinned at the child. 'What's all the noise for, eh? We're just going on a little journey, that's all.'
This didn't help matters; the little boy just bawled even louder, and squirmed in his mother's arms – she was red with embarrassment and fury. She struggled on, dumped the stroller in the rack and sat down. Taylor paid for both of us, then we stood towards the front. He looked down the length of the packed bus, then said in a low voice,
'Will you look at all these guys! Every one of them unhappy and apprehensive and sullen, even on a day like this. They look as if they're off to their own funerals.'
'It's probably the thought of having to go into town at this hour, and struggling through all the crowds trying to go the other way.'
'Yeah, but why need it be a struggle? It's just the way they see it, Dan. They're thinking something along the lines of, oh Hell,

another day of fighting and misery and screaming kids and people who don't understand me, and they can't see that they can change their situation just by seeing what they have in a different light'.

The bus crawled towards Reading Bridge. For some reason, there was a lot of traffic going towards the centre, although nothing was coming the other way. The driver was grumbling to himself.
'Bloody traffic. Wonder who's had an accident up ahead this time?'
His two-way radio crackled.
'137, where are you?'
'Coming up to Reading Bridge. There's a lot of traffic going in. Got a full load as well.'
We inched along the road. Glancing up the bus, I suddenly saw, right at the back, the fucking weirdo again. He looked back at me and smiled briefly, before burying his head in his notebook once more. I pointed him out to Taylor.
'I think he's following us.'
'Why should he?' he said. 'Just because he was in the same pub and now on the same bus doesn't mean anything.'
'I don't know. He keeps looking at me, that's all'.
I rolled and unrolled my ticket and glanced at what was written on it – time, destination, fare, jolly little 'have a nice journey' message. The bus wheezed over the bridge; Some teenagers were busy throwing themselves off it and into the dark waters of the Thames below. A few swans and geese bobbed on its surface and a cruiser slid towards the lock.
'The Thames,' murmured Taylor. 'Did you know that in Old British it means 'Dark River'? When the Romans were first up in this part of the world, they thought this was the Styx'.
Our busload of souls were ferried over it, then, and finally we arrived at the station, pulling up to the festering monstrosity that is the Station Tower. Someone had obviously decided to start their weekend festivities early, as a great puddle of vomit lay outside the chicken kebab shop. Skirting it, I said, 'well, we know where not to eat on the way back then.'
There was a waft of stale piss from the doorway of the Jolly Porter, and stale rank air rising from the depths of Bar Oz.

Outside the old Foster Wheeler building, a huddle of office workers in rumpled shirts sucked upon their fags before going back to work for the final stretch of the day, that miserable last hour and a half before you can reasonably escape the drudgery of the week, then go and get drunk for the weekend. We crossed towards the station and I bought some more cigarettes from W H Smiths.

'Where now, Dan?'

'There's the Three Guineas next to this, or the Forum over the road, but I'm not keen on either. How about the Blagrave round the corner?'

'Lead on – you know this place better than me'.

We crossed the station concourse, past great packs of tourists and language school students, all of who were trying to put as many miles between them and Reading as possible. We came out by the Railair bus link, skirted a coach being filled with luggage and people destined for Heathrow and crossed the road again, round the corner and into the Blagrave. A few years ago, it was a real London-type spit - and - sawdust; There were etched glass windows and cut mirrors behind the bar; dark mahogany furniture and even gas lighting. Now, it has almost perpetual sport on and electric, but it's OK as town pubs go. The one good thing about it was its sense of peace – it was essentially one of those bars that has a feeling of serenity around it. At this time of day, it was sparsely populated, and those who were there looked like they'd been at it since the doors opened. A few seemed to have been occupying the same place since the pub was built. Despite the brightness of the open air, little light filtered through the panes, leaving it all in perpetual half-light. This was probably just as well considering some of the more decrepit specimens of drinker. I went for a piss while Taylor got the drinks in. I thought about what he had said so far, or rather, what he hadn't; Neither of us, in fact, had said much, but I was damned if I could think of a reason why that should be so. We hadn't seen each other for so long, surely we would have far, far more to talk about. I remembered an evening on the beach in Goa, where we had sat and conversed about life, love, politics, metaphysics, God and God knows what all night, and all the time we were laughing our heads off. And right now, it seemed strangely disjointed, as if we were on slightly different levels of communication. Then again, we were both older, and I had only recently begun to notice how much I had changed, much to my chagrin; I had to admit that I wasn't immortal any more, that I would become decrepit and die just like everyone else. That is the really hard part of being in the mid-thirties – accepting that one day you will die, and I was bang slap in the middle of the change: Perhaps Taylor had something like that on his mind, too, although it was hard to imagine him turning middle-aged. He was one of those friends you expect to produce brilliant, wild, inspiring thoughts and writings, then one day just cease to be, leaving only a brilliant after-image on the retina of the mind, a glowing thought and memento of youth. In a way, he had died for me on that evening in Beirut.

Now he was back. And what was this about Beattie? My heart had lurched when he mentioned her name, and how on earth had he found her? It seemed unlikely that he could possibly have tracked her down in Bangkok of all places, but then again, I wouldn't put it past his abilities. It seemed to me that this evening was going to be one full of ghosts.

When I came back to the bar, there was Taylor, but, it suddenly seemed to me, the Old Taylor, the brilliant, flashing, incisive poetic one, laughing and in full flow with two old blokes. They were talking animatedly. One of the men was short, bearded and spectacularly ugly, with an enormous buckled red nose, viciously protruding teeth, all at different angles, and a scrunched, gnomish face, and the other was slightly taller and red-faced, bearded too and beaming at his companion. They were obviously both off their faces on Guinness and whisky. Taylor handed me an ale.

'Dan, meet two friends of mine', he laughed. 'Plato and Socrates.'

I must have looked surprised, because they both laughed.

'Socrates O'Toole and Plato Jones', said Socrates (obviously, the uglier one), 'Bar philosophers and pundits and what you will.'

'We have other names, you see, but these are our noms de guerre for our forays into the wide world,' said Plato.

'Provided the world exists', said Socrates. 'Prove it'.

'Gah, give me enough beers and I'll prove anything', Plato retorted. 'Talking of which...?'

'James! James, me good lad…..another pair of whiskies if you will….bless you..'
The barman poured out a pair, and Socrates turned to me again.
'We were just having a good laugh at your friend's expense here', he said, breathing wheezily.
'Yes, I heard Plato here shout 'Socrates!' and I couldn't help laughing', explained Taylor, 'then they ask my name and hail me as the poet'.
'And what's your name, if I may enquire?' asked Plato.
'Dan Thompson.'
'What's that?', roared Socrates. 'Dante?'
'No, Dan T….'
'Oh yes, oh yes, that's good!', laughed Plato. 'Look here, will you Socrates, Dante and the dead poet!'
They both chuckled and wheezed, while Taylor grinned into his drink. When the laughter had subsided into the wheeze that old men reach after a while, Socrates turned to me, wiped a rheumy tear from his eye, and asked,
'Well? Is it true then? Are you following your guide through Hell? And how far have you come?'
'Em, well, I thought we were just going for a few beers myself.'
Plato tugged Socrates' sleeve.
'If that is true, that means we're in Limbo, does it not?'
'Well, if so, at least we won't be toasted by the big fellow, you know?'
'And anyway,' said Taylor, 'This is Dan's town. I'm a stranger here.'
'Only in the physical sense, maybe,' muttered Socrates. 'There is the sense around you that you know where you're going, young man, whereas you,' he pointed his bulbous nose at me, 'are somewhat lost. Am I right?'
I gave a shrug, but he had discomfited me. Was it so obvious?
'Direction. Always have a direction in life, that's my advice,' said Plato.
'Our direction, for example, has led us to here', said Socrates, and they laughed.
'Yes, yes, we're all of us philosophers of the pub, poets of the pint, and crapulous pundits of the world in here,' Plato chuckled, to a murmured 'yes' from his companion. 'For most of

us, we never saw the light properly, mainly because it was being seen through the bottom of a pint glass, see?'

He pointed at the various piles of old men sat around in the twilight.

'The one with the wooden leg and the row of medals? War hero – lost his wife a few years back. That chap in the tan cap used to be mayor of Reading, don't you know...'

Someone started singing. Badly.

'..he's a folk singer, that one, and over there is a very great gentleman.'

Socrates snorted into his drink. 'Great, my arse! A good reporter as was, more like'.

Seated at the far end of the bar was a rotund, short man with heavy jowls, eyes that stuck out somewhat, a few strands of hair on his round head, and jaundiced skin.

'Newspaperman. Reported on conflicts and whatnot,' said Plato. 'Of course, his liver's gone, hence the colour on him. And he's blind – blind drunk!'

As we watched, the man knocked back his beer in one go, then slipped off his stool, accompanied by a kind of 'doh' sound. The barman came round, propped him back on, and he nodded forward until his head touched the bar and he fell asleep.

'Ah, there we go, he's nodded off,' said Socrates. 'They'll leave him be till the wife comes in and picks him up'.

'In a wheelbarrow.'

'Speaking of such, Plato, what time do you have? The wife'll be after me before long.'

'Time for a few more, time for a few more.' He turned to us. 'Poor Socrates here has a hard time in store for himself later, you see. His other half doesn't comprehend that philosophising requires frequent refreshment.'

We finished off our beers and made to go.

'A pleasure to meet you,' said Taylor.

'And you, O poet', beamed Socrates. 'And you, young man. Stop looking so downcast. Things will get better soon. Off with you.'

'Bye.'

We came out of the pub into the dusty light. Office workers were beginning to stumble from their offices, either heading for home or for the bars. We crossed the road towards the Town Hall, an edifice of gothic styles in red brick.

'That's quite a funky building,' commented Taylor.
'Yeah, the guy who built it also did the Natural History Building…there's the 3 B's in it, but unless you want to repeat the drunk pensioner experience I suggest we leave it for now.'
'You know best.'
We walked past it to the square that leads to Market place and the Forbury. St. Laurence's was, as ever, closed, and from its tower medieval gargoyles leered the length of Friar Street. We stopped under the statue of Victoria while I tried to make up my mind which way to go. The pubs along Friar Street didn't appeal at this time of day; Generally, they'd be filled with weary shoppers and perpetual drunks. As I was debating with myself, we suddenly heard a great roar and screech, and around the corner came tottering a group of young women, yelling and giggling. In the middle of them was a twenty-something woman, wearing a bridal veil, a pair of fake tits, furry handcuffs and an L-plate.
'It's a bit early for a hen night, isn't it?' asked Taylor.
'This is Reading on a Friday,' I replied. 'It's never too early for anything.'
There was another shout then, but this came from the alleyway between the church and Blandy and Blandy's offices. A troupe of young men staggered into sight, half-carrying one of their number; He too was wearing an L-Plate and a pair of fake tits, and he feebly waved a plastic ball and chain.
'Dave! Dave!' bellowed one. 'When's the 'Oneypot open?'
'Not 'till seven', yelled Dave, who was lanky, spotty and red-faced. 'Let's go to Burger King and get something to eat before we go on.'
The two groups saw each other.
'Alright ladies? Going anywhere nice?' drawled one of the party. A few of the women giggled, the one bellowed, 'Sod the chat, get it out!'
'Yeah, show us yer cock!'
'One at a time and later on, yeah?' someone else shouted back, and the two parties slipped laughing past each other. The women walked straight past us on their way towards O'Neill's, the Irish Bar. The bride-to be slipped and fell right into me with a loud 'whoops!' I helped her back up onto her feet.
'There you go,'

'Ta. I'm getting' married tomorrow', she said.
'Really?! I'd never have noticed',
'Yeah', she replied, with the sudden seriousness of the very drunk, 'My Gary. Met him at school .'
She looked directly into my face, and gripped me at the elbows, as if trying to make me comprehend entirely what she meant, her face serious, her brow buckled. 'I love him! I really, really love him!'
And then she started crying. Her friend peeled her off me, saying 'Come on Fran, yeah, let's have another drink...' She turned to me. 'Sorry 'bout that.'
'That's OK – tell her to be careful, yeah?'
And then they whirled away and were swallowed by the pub's dark mouth.
'Well, They're off in that direction. Let's try this way, it's probably quieter,' said Taylor, and he turned left towards Market Place. I followed on.

FIVE: a vision

Report of activity recorded on CCTV in Reading Town Centre, July the --, ----.

3.55 p.m. camera 5, Station Hill: The view outside Forbuoys Newsagents. The number 137 bus enters the picture. It stops, and several people alight from it: An elderly woman, with white hair, walking stick and floral print dress; A woman of approximately 30 years of age, with a young child in a pushchair, wearing a yellow top and white shorts; One middle-aged Asian man, approximately forty to fifty years of age, wearing a light grey suit; Two teenage girls, wearing light-coloured tops and shorts; An elderly couple in beige; And last, two men, in their thirties, one of whom was approximately five feet eleven inches tall, with greying dark brown hair, wearing a dark t-shirt and jeans, and the other several inches taller, with long black hair, white shirt and dark trousers. These latter two walked towards the station.

3.58 p.m. camera 7, station concourse: The two men enter the picture via the station entrance of W.H. Smiths. They are seen to stop briefly in front of the information board, apparently to check the time. A man carrying a suitcase can be seen falling over behind them, but they do not appear to notice. They walk towards the far end of the concourse, past the Reading College and School of Art and Design Pavilion. The taller man turns and smiles at a woman in her mid-twenties wearing a short blue dress. She returns the smile. The shorter man walks on. He is apparently talking, although about what is not clear. His companion smiles and nods. They leave the concourse via the southeast exit.

3.59 p.m. camera 8, station and railbus: The two are seen coming down the stairs. The shorter one slips, but regains his composure. They walk around the side of the 4.15 railbus departure and are lost to view.

3.59 p.m. camera 11, corner of Station approach and Blagrave street: the two men walk slowly towards the corner. The shorter of the two gestures in front of him; his companion smiles and shrugs. Having passed the corner, they enter The Blagrave public house.

4.32 p.m. , camera 11, corner of Station approach and Blagrave street: The two men are seen leaving the Blagrave public house, and heading up Blagrave street. They cross the road towards the Old Town Hall, then walk up to the square. They stop under the statue of Queen Victoria, and are the seen to look to their left.

4.35 p.m., camera 13, St. Laurence's and Market Place junction: A party of women, all aged between approximately eighteen and forty, are seen to enter the square from the east. It could be said that they are in high spirits, and it may be surmised that they have been drinking. Shortly after, a party of men, all aged approximately in their twenties, enter the square via the alleyway that runs between St. Laurence's church and Blandy & Blandy, solicitors. One young man is apparently the worse for wear, being supported by his companions. The two parties converge and converse briefly, but without any incident of note. The party of men then proceed westwards up Friar Street, while the group of females heads towards the Irish Bar on the corner of Friar Street and Blagrave Street. One woman, aged approximately in her twenties, stumbles and falls onto the shorter of the two men being thus far observed, appears to talk to him briefly, before being assisted into the bar by her companion. The taller of the two men then heads eastward and turns the corner into Market Place, followed by his companion.

And all the while this narrow view is going on? Men and women walk through the streets, living, working, crying, whatever; A few pigeons roam the square, and are chased by a delighted two-year-old boy; there are beggars on the corners, lazily asking for spare change; a traffic warden writes out a ticket for a badly-parked car by the church, and a woman comes racing toward him, screaming curses before getting in her vehicle and driving off; a woman in her forties looks out of the window of the solicitors and sighs; three girls, two Slovaks and a Pole, come out of the private language school on the corner and chat as they walk towards Marks & Spensers; And all the time there is bustle and movement and life and God knows what that a single eye can't take in or understand.

Six: The well-worn quote

If I'm drunk on forbidden wine, so I am!
And if I'm an unbeliever, a pagan or idolater, so I am!
Every sect has its own suspicions of me,
I myself am just what I am.

Omar Khayyam, Ruba'iyat LXXIV

In which the Author continues to interrupt the narrative; He comments briefly on the action thus far and what may be expected later; And discusses the use of prefatory quotes and summary paragraphs, as well as authorial interruptions, for their ability to pad out and impart greater gravitas to even the weakest of stories.

It would appear that I am still on the bus, it seems – or at least, my presence in the town has not been commented upon by Dan. This poses a problem: If I am not there, who's writing the story? It resembles something out of Zen philosophy, does it not? You see, it does not matter how clever the writer is at disguising him- or herself, the Authorial Hand is still present and detectable in even the most well-written internal monologue. Just as the single word can contain multitudes of meaning, so the text can be pared back, layer after layer, to reveal the writer and their naked mind.

This is why I have decided to jump into the narrative as a character (or, perhaps later, characters) in my own right; I may be in the background, but I'm the idiot waving and jumping, the boy pointing out that the Emperor has no clothes on, the clown pointing the obvious fact: *this is a fiction*. Likewise, being the fool in the court, I may safely wade into the middle of the action and bring it to a crashing halt while I pontificate on what I like. And the joy is, this too is fiction! Yes, I admit it; I am a character myself, and one that is increasing in strength as this tale unfolds. So who's pulling *my* strings?

You also have to decide something, dear reader: Which is the real narrative?

I don't know about you, but Socrates' outburst about Dante took me by surprise. Is this whole story really just a gloss on

Inferno from The Comedy? Is it, in short, blatant theft? Well, I am going to deal with the pernicious, mendacious nature of tales in a later interruption. If it is a gloss, why? Is Reading a comic version of Hell? Is the story a comedy? Of course, comedy in its original sense meant a story with a happy outcome. Right now, I'll settle for Dan managing to get back home safe and unmolested (unless, of course, he wants to be molested), which technically means it's a comedy. I've not intended to have dead bodies all over the place, although it may inject a bit of zest into it, don't you think? Let's face it, two men on a pub crawl is hardly enthralling is it? And I must say, I'm not particularly impressed by my own conjuration of the town and environs so far – there doesn't seem to be much detail. Must try harder. And Taylor Coleridge is somewhat of a mystery still – he seems rather taciturn, despite Dan's assertion that his friend was back on form while talking with the bar sages. However, we must take into account the fact that the narrative is from a personal perspective, and it could be that Dan is not a particularly observant chap. Let us see what happens next – I daresay it will involve more pubs. They have added one more beer each to their respective tallies, and it isn't even five o'clock yet. I hope they can last this kind of pace until two in the morning, but then, what does it matter! This is fiction! And, by the way, I'm not too sure about this use of a CCTV's perspective – contrived, maybe, and for what purpose?

 There is also the matter of these interludes, the absurd chapter titles, the introductory quotes and the chapter summaries – why? Well, and I answer – why not? I've already explained that I can do as I like in terms of narrative interruption, and I won't explain that further. The other stuff – can it be explained or justified? Well, the chapter summaries have an ancient and noble history in the rise of the English novel, and have been of immense value to those people who are generally far too busy to read any given novel in full – in short, those whose lives are so ostensibly rich and varied that they do not need the vapid joys of a novel or a soap opera on TV. They merely need to flick through each chapter heading, get the gist of the thing, and claim to have read the book from start to finish. This is why, and only those who have actually read this will know it, that from now on the chapter summaries will be unfaithful to what is actually in each chapter: some may be accurate, but you will not be able to rely on them hence. There, that's you warned.

As for the quotes – well, they give a bit of class, don't they? I must admit, they're more of a continental affectation, but anything to puff the whole story up. Quotes, preferably by foreign writers and preferably in foreign, are nothing more than a bit of gilding, an ornate and unnecessary adornment to the text. For that reason, I have added them – they just look good, and give the reader the impression that the Author is far more erudite and well-read than is the real case. For example, take the quote at the head of this chapter – taken from the Ruba'iyat of Omar Khayyam. Let's see- what buttons does it push? Foreign writer – good; Islamic Sufi Mystic – good as well; verse number written in Roman Numerals – excellent. And what is its relationship to this chapter? Nothing. Nada. Zilch. Not a sausage. Not even a small pork chipolata on a cocktail stick. With a bit of pineapple. And a cheese cube.

But it still looks good. Why is this? Because you have been conditioned, dear reader; conditioned by the types of book you read to believe that, if there are quotes regularly sprinkled in a text, it must necessarily be LITERATURE. The fact is, these fripperies, these added-on extras, rather than being seen for the nonsense they are, somehow convey an added factor to any book – that precious and August thing, Gravitas. A book fully decked out in its costume of summaries, notes, and quotes grasps the attention. Quite possibly, it also has an introduction, which may be written by someone who isn't a friend of the Author. It may even be required reading in schools and colleges, and for which reason, it begins to resemble the Queen: Admired from afar, but never touched.

This is obviously nonsense, and, like the summaries, from now on expect the quotes to become equally unhinged from the story –they may be relevant, they may have an inner truth pertaining to the tale, they may be arrant nonsense – but just don't rely on them. I might even make some up and attribute them to non-existent Great Foreign Writers.

Seven: The hungry and the spent

The best lack all conviction, whilst the worst are full of passionate intensity.

                                                        W.B. Yeats

In which our heroes do something. Or not, as the case may be.

Once we got round the corner, I suggested the Cooper's, but Taylor said,
'Let's lay off for a bit, shall we? We've got all evening ahead. Is there a coffee shop hereabouts?'
'OK, there's one right ahead.'
We walked past Nino's, the Italian restaurant that had been in Butter Market ever since I could remember. The door opened and a gush of aromas, of tomato and olive oil and herbs and hot bread raced out, then disappeared quickly as the door was shut behind two diners entering the fragrant maw. Under the plane trees, pigeons vied and fluttered over bread crumbs that were being flung by an elderly Indian woman. A couple of drunks were sat on one of the benches, with cans of cheap cider between them. One was dozing, the other muttering to himself and taking great thirsty gulps from his drink. Suddenly, a huge dog came out of nowhere and dived among the pigeons, barking and snapping. I'm not sure what kind of hound it was – something like a pit bull terrier, but much, much bigger and darker. The pigeons scattered and whirled into the trees and the dog began looking for something else to chase. Fortunately, its owner came chasing after it – the thing had slipped his grasp. Not surprising, really; Like many people who own huge dogs, he was a rather weedy specimen in a tracksuit and baseball cap.
'Trevor! Come 'ere!' The man chased Trevor, who took delight in running around him in circles and knocking over some of the cider cans by the drunks' feet. Finally, the man grabbed hold of it.
'Trevor! Heel! Bloody dog…! Stop it…STOP! Stupid sodding animal….sorry 'bout that, mate, no 'arm done, yeah? Great…Trevor!'
And off he was dragged by Trevor.

We walked past the old cafeteria: for a Friday afternoon on a hot day, it was surprisingly full. It smelt, as ever, of warm milky coffee and hot vinegar and fatty fried things, which were its speciality. Inside, people wolfed down their food, although they didn't seem to be getting much pleasure from it. Outside Costa Coffee on the corner of Broad Street and Butter Market, there was a spare table which we blagged. A waitress, a Polish girl I guessed, judging by the name (Agnieska) on her nametag, took our order. I pulled out a cigarette and squinted across the street at the crowds flowing like so much seawater into and out of the Oracle.

'Why is that shopping centre called the Oracle? It's a bloody stupid name', said Taylor.

'There used to be a poorhouse cum slave labour factory called the same around there during the sixteen hundreds or something', I replied. 'If you go to the museum, it's still got the doors in it'.

Taylor's eyes glittered and a grim smile worked its way across his face.

'And now it's a temple selling the products of slavery and sweat.'

'Well, irony has never been something the good citizens of Reading have ever appreciated, especially when it comes to money', I said. 'Most of the riots we've had here historically have been about profits and who controls the dosh. A Reading version of a dictionary would probably define irony as something that resembles iron.'

'Now imagine', he said, 'Imagine that this really is a temple, say a modern version of something at Delphi. And inside it is some mad priestess woman, crazed on purchasing consumer delights, frenzied as the prophetess of Pythian Apollo after drinking from the sacred well, and she's giving all sorts of mad pronouncements. Buy This! Don't Buy That! Special Bargains! Imagine all these people going in, receiving her wild talk and coming out dazed and terrified by what they had encountered!'

'Well, there's the information counter.'

We both laughed, and Agnieska brought us our coffees.

'dzien koye', Taylor said in Polish. The girl smiled broadly and said,

'Oh, you know Polish! Very good!'

'No, only 'thank you' I'm afraid. Oh, and 'kapuska'', to which she laughed, then went back inside. 'That means cabbage', he explained.
'So how did you know she's Polish?'
'And you mean you didn't? I took an educated guess, as you did, I suspect. Besides, if I'd got it wrong, she'd have gently disabused me at best or ignored me at worst. Look around you, Dan! Don't just guess at stuff: act upon what you know, or think you know. What have you got to lose?'
'Yeah, alright. I've done it before – you know that, that's why I went abroad in the first place. Just to see what's out there, see if I could do it, you know, work, live abroad and so on. Alright, so I don't have your way with languages, Taylor, but I did it, didn't I? And now I'm back here.'
'You say that like you're disappointed to be back. And that attitude means you never went away. You know Dan, I seem to remember a conversation we had like this before – do you recall that coffee house in Cairo, all those Hookahs outside and we two getting merrily stoned on them?'
It came to mind then; a sunny afternoon in late January or early February in a small street in that city, and Taylor and me sitting on small stools, a hookah each and tulip glasses of sweet, hot tea.
'We were swapping tales, and talking about what we mean by 'home' and 'away'', I said.
'And remember, you said that home is something that is always in the heart and soul – you can't escape it', he said. 'Then we decided that the level of pessimism of the soul decides whether home is a good thing or something to try and run away from, but that you cannot run away from your heart, and so you carry home with you wherever you go'.
'Christ, we must have really been puffing on those hookahs by then!' It was a weak joke, and just bluster really.
'Don't be so feeble. Look you're complaining about being here, but why? You said yourself, another time, that going abroad was like leaving a cage didn't you?'
I shrugged my assent. It was true; Like many British people who escape this island, abroad had seemed an incredibly liberating action.

'Now you're back in the cage. But I'm here asking: Is it really a cage, or is that just the way you choose to see it?'
He sipped his coffee and watched me.
I laughed, but an exasperated laugh.
'Well, what the Hell do you expect me to say to that, man?'
'Nothing, Dan. Nothing at all. Relax, enjoy the coffee and look around.'
 And so I did. It had gone five by now, and I watched the world carefully over my coffee and cigarettes. Next to us were a couple of men with olive-dark skin, arguing in what sounded like Turkish; the waitress was talking animatedly in Polish with another girl; A man with short dark hair and glasses walked by, carrying a copy of El Pais; A pair of middle aged women, dressed in shalwar kameez walked within earshot, chatting and laughing in Punjabi. I saw a group of Chinese students, obviously coming back out of the college, shouting and laughing, then three girls speaking French. Over our cigarettes and the next five minutes, Taylor and I watched the world go by. Such a rush of people, and so many nationalities. I counted fifteen different languages in that time.
Taylor put out his fag.
'So why go out into the big bad world', he said finally, 'when it seems to be so eager to come to Reading?'
He grinned.
'I'm getting to like this place. How many people live here, then?'
'I'm not sure. Not that many. About a hundred and seventy thousand.'
'A medium sized town, then. But did you just see how many languages are being spoken? That's quite something.'
'I can't say I'd really noticed before'.
'Then it's time you opened your eyes and ears a bit! Look at this place. It's as lively as any souk , market or bazaar we've been to, and I'll bet it's a damn sight more cosmopolitan too. Just because it doesn't happen to be abroad doesn't mean it's any less interesting. Here we are, sat in a coffee house, and they're the natural place for stories. Think of how many you could conjure just by sitting here. Anyway...'
He drained his coffee.
'I need a piss. Shall we proceed to the next watering hole?'
'Why not? The Hobgoblin's next door.'

'Sounds good to me.'

We paid for our coffees, and stood up to move on. As we did so, one of the local beggars, a man with badly-shorn short hair, tangled beard and with an equally bedraggled-looking hound on a string walked towards us and muttered something.

'I'm sorry?' said Taylor.

The beggar muttered again and stretched out his hand.

'I don't understand what you're saying, but the answer's 'no' anyway',' he answered. Then the beggar, as far as I could see through his beard, went red, then clenched his fists before stomping off.

We wandered into the dark and stale interior of the Hobgoblin. Taylor went off to the bogs, and I got the drinks in at the tiny bar. Apart from the darkness, the whole place was sticky from the floor up, the testament of years of Real Ale drinking and copious smoking. The ceilings were a thick yellow. The air was a comforting fuggy mix of stale beer, staler carpet and ashtrays. The bar consisted of a few tables and chairs, all in dark, cracked wood, then a row of tiny cubicles that gave the place an air of antiquity, although I knew that it had only been done up like that in the 1990's. A few office workers were perched on the windowsills and bench outside the front; Inside, the noise level was beginning to crank up as people started to leave work and come for a beer or ten. In one corner, some guy who'd obviously decided to give up for the day at lunchtime, judging by his red, sweaty face and the way he was swaying, was chunking his money into the fruit machine and cursing half to himself. He gave the start button slap after great big slap, and thumped the machine each time it swallowed a pound without giving a return. The nudge buttons flashed, and he'd stand on tiptoe to peer into the bowels of the machine and try to work out which symbols were on the reels, then crouch down and look upwards for the same purpose. All his concentration was fixed on trying to win, most likely just the money he'd already put in the thing. Taylor came back, and we got a seat next to the window. We supped our beers in silence for a while as we watched Mr. Gambler get more and more infuriated with the machine. He ran out of cash at one point: He put his last thirty pence in it, then slugged back his beer and went to the bar. He slapped a twenty pound note on the bar.

'I'll have another, thanks. And can I have the change in coins?'
One beer and a handful of metal later, he fed all the money into the machine and began his frenzied squinting and slapping again. Taylor smiled over his beer at this.
'Fruit machines are bloody stupid.'
'Only if you're the mug playing them.'
' True. Look at this poor bastard here – he's so obsessed with the idea of winning, he doesn't even notice that he's already lost.'
Gambling Man was clearly getting angrier and angrier. He scowled, he patted, he coaxed, he cursed. But it made no difference.
'You'll see, he'll give up, then someone'll come along, put in fifty pence or whatever and clean it out. Then he'll be back another day, and the same thing will happen.'
'Hope springs eternal'.
'There's a difference between being optimistic and just being an idiot', retorted Taylor. 'This bloke just doesn't know when to admit defeat. That's the problem with luck, I guess; Never comes when you want it to, and when it does, it's never exactly what you expect'.
'So was it luck you found Beattie, then?'
Taylor paused, had a drink, looked straight at me, and smiled.
'Of course it was. It wasn't as if I'd specifically gone off in search of her. There's a phrase, something about how chance favours someone who's well-prepared. You ever heard something like that?'
I hadn't. He waved his hand, and continued.
'Whatever, you mentioned in one of your last emails that you thought she was in Indonesia or Malaysia or something. I knew what she looked like, and I knew she worked as an English teacher. You see – I was prepared, in a way, and chance happened. I was in Bangkok; I was walking along Khao San Road, where, as you know, most foreigners and would-be teachers congregate; and I was walking past a bar, when we both know how much English teachers drink; and there she was. The lucky meeting happened in part because of preparation.'
'Now that's clever, Taylor, and I'd have done the same, but I wouldn't have come across her, given the same circumstances.'

'That's because, right now, you're looking through the glass darkly. You don't expect anything good to happen to you right now. You don't think you're going to find the crock of gold. And you know what? That hurts. Here I am – isn't this something good?'

And he opened his arms and grinned broadly.

There was a sudden, loud 'FUCK!' from Mr. Gambler as his money finally ran out. He finished his beer, then waddled off to the toilet.

'Watch this', said Taylor, and he went up to the fruit machine and put in a coin. He pressed the start button a couple of times, then pressed the nudge buttons, then he gambled, and started grinning broadly. Two minutes later, he pressed collect, and out clunked twenty-five pounds.

'See? Fortune favours patience and preparation. Someone puts twenty quid in – hell, it's got to be worth putting the pound in, even if you just get that back. Well, that'll pay for a few more beers.'

At this point, Gambling Man, returned, got another beer and lumbered back to the machine.

'I'm not going to tell him', Taylor said, gulped his beer, and we both lit up our fags.

We watched the late afternoon crowds slowly change composition, from mothers with young children and older people, all dressed in casual clothes, to people in suits and formal wear tottering into the humid streets from the rarefied air-conditioned climes of their offices, then heading towards home or bar. Friday night was coming, and time to play. The pub crowd swelled and spilled onto the pavement, a swarm of relaxed post-work nattering, and there was the choppy susurrus of talk and laughter. The street echoed with the clatter of footfalls and the sound of passing traffic heading towards the Oracle and Castle Street.

'Now notice him', Taylor suddenly said. He gestured towards a far corner, where sat a guy of about the same age as us, alone. He was counting his money, then looking at his pint, which he was gripping for dear life, then looking at his money again and sighing.

'Now he is the antithesis of our fat chum here', he continued, 'too damn frightened to let go and enjoy himself or spend his money at all.'
'He might just be skint.'
'He's sat there since we came in and has had two sips of his beer, and he's got enough on him for another. He opened his wallet and counted what he had a few minutes ago.'
'So he doesn't want to spend.'
'Exactly! He's a tightfist. Why else is he on his own? He's done nothing but sit by himself, stare at his solitary beer, sigh and count his cash. If you have money, spend it –that's what it's there for – but don't throw it away. Fat machine man just made me twenty quid richer, and now I'm going to spend it sensibly, on alcohol.'
'Good idea. Another one here, then move on?'
'Why not?'
As Taylor went to the bar, Mr. Fruit Machine erupted again and gave the thing a thump. He stomped around, and lurched for the bar, but was evidently a bit too pissed, because as he negotiated round the crowd he crashed straight into the tightfist's table, not only spilling his drink but also scattering all the coins that he had carefully been stacking on the top.
'Oh shit! Sorry mate!' The beer had spilled all over the guy's crotch. He leaped up, furious.
'Look what you've done! And me money all over the floor!'
'Sorry...what was it you were drinking, eh?'
The tightfist subsided into grumbles and whines, but was eventually placated by a pint of beer – in fact, probably a more expensive beer than he'd had previously.
 It was gradually getting warmer and more humid inside, and the beer was flowing easily by now, as was the talk. Taylor and I chatted about our travels, about the various bars we'd been to and with whom – easy flowing banter, charming and pointless in the warmth. Eventually, we hauled ourselves out.
'Right, which way now?'
'How about the Turks? I haven't been there for a while. It's that direction.'
We crossed the street to The George Hotel, then down Kings Street, past Mothercare and Burger King, then we turned into Duke Street. A welcome gust of wind took the edge off the heat,

but scattered dust and litter and old newspapers. Walking towards the bridge, we saw a small group of beggars, huddled into the porch of the old Ship hotel. A couple of them were just lying on the floor, staring up at the ceiling: three others were sitting and drinking and bickering fiercely with each other. One of the supine, an utterly miserable looking woman, was mouthing silent words into the air rhythmically and repetitively. Her arguing companions were obviously covering some very well-worn topic, something concerning who had taken what from whom and done what to somebody else, and each of the three had taken entrenched positions. They gestured and shouted, then fell into glowering exhausted silence, then reiterate what they had just said. They'd probably been going on about the same thing for months.

LETTERS

Reading Evening Post, July __, ____. Send letters addressed to the Editor to the Reading Post, Richfield Avenue, Reading. Emails must contain a name and address, which can be withheld on request.

Letter of the day

Regarding Councillor Knotwood's suggestion for a new hostel for the homeless in Silver Street, I feel I must speak up. I am not one to write to newspapers in general, nor am I one to complain, but I have to stand up and be counted on this issue. We do not need a homeless hostel in the centre of Reading, and certainly not in Silver Street where I and many other elderly and respectable residents live. It is not a case of "not in my back yard". I would not want to inflict this home and its crime-prone inhabitants on anyone living in our town. There are enough beggars as it is. They are a shocking sight on the streets and are frequently aggressive and dangerous. No wonder businesses look elsewhere when they want to set up headquarters, and it is little surprise that we have so few tourists.

If we must have homeless hostels, why not put them on former military bases, which are far from our town centres? Then they would get a job soon enough.

Mr. Bob Gouge
Silver Street
Reading

Swimming in memories

I would like to say thank you, Evening Post, for printing the old photograph of the King's Meadow Lido (June 30th). It brought back many happy memories for me, especially as I can be seen in the far left of the picture, wearing the striped bathing costume. I and my friends, Dolly Watson and Margery Toodod, who have both sadly passed away recently, spent almost every day of summer there when we were children. It is such a shame it had to close – but perhaps now it will be restored to its former glory, instead of the vandalised shell it is. Thank you.

Dorothy (Dot) Mathersley
Mander Court

Reading

Hunting rage

I, along with many of the citizens of Reading, enjoy the traditional pursuits of fishing and hunting. They are rights that all English people are entitled to, through centuries of fighting for them. Yet I feel I speak for the silent majority when I say that this government has gone far too far in pushing for a total ban on hunting. I was one of many who protested outside the House of Commons on this issue, and I was shocked by the behaviour of our police forces. I always thought they were there to enforce the letter of the law, not trample on our freedoms. Our protest was friendly and civil, yet they treated us as though we were the worst kind of anarchists and revolutionaries. First this government sells us to Europe, and now it is creating the absolutely worst kind of socialist dictatorship to oppress all right thinking people. I know, and am sure, that the people of Reading will speak as one voice and vote this government out at the next election.

Sue Stout
Councillor, UKIP
Highdown Close
Emmer Green
Reading

Loopy idea

Has the Borough Council gone stark raving mad? I refer to their scheme to make the Inner Distribution Road a one way route. Not only would it make the already terrible traffic situation worse, it would also add forty-five minutes to my journey to work during the rush hour. Come on, council – do something right with my council tax money for once. How about widening the roads?

Nigel Chadwick
Via email

Thanks a ton

I would like to say a big 'thank you' via your letters page to the lady who helped me to my feet last Friday. I was carrying my shopping through Smelly Alley when I stumbled on a loose paving slab and fell to the ground. As I am quite a large lady, and am on disability benefit because of my size, I could not lift myself up, and lay there in some distress for several minutes, while people walked around me. Fortunately, there are some Good Samaritans in Reading, and the lady in the floral dress with short blond hair helped me up. Bless you, and I hope your back is better.

I also think the council should do something concerning paving slabs.

Name Withheld.

Stop knocking our town!

Alright, we all know that Reading isn't the most beautiful or exciting city in the whole wide world, but is that an excuse to always be making fun of it? I find myself getting increasingly annoyed these days at those who think it's fine to rib us or put us down. So we have terrible traffic – so does London. So we have drug abuse and related crime – show me a place that doesn't. So we don't have much in the way of picturesque and historical buildings – isn't everywhere the same these days? So our idea of entertainment is either snooker at the Hexagon or getting drunk for the whole weekend – tell me how that's different from other towns in the region. So the centre is virtually hostage to teenagers and hooligans every Friday and Saturday night – what's new?

Look at what we do have – enviable transport links, easy access to the capital, and picturesque countryside just outside the town, as well as the Thames and Kennet – and, of course, the wonders of the Oracle shopping centre itself. So come on – let's stick up for Our Town, and tell the jokers where to go!

Bill Laud
Kendrick Road
Reading

Eight: Reading is Hell

Fowler's ministry did not last long, for he had many enemies among the Anglicans, one of whom called him "the author of most of the evil in the town"…some years later he was succeeded by the Rev Thomas Juice….

Daphne Phillips, The Story of Reading

And so Dan and Taylor creep towards the Turk's Head in London Road as the sun begins to set. I am actually following at some distance behind them, hence the reason why Dan hasn't seen me for a while. When the breeze blew, it flung the above part of the newspaper at me, which I have decided to include. It's interesting, isn't it, how the letters page of a local paper tells you so much of the people of a town. An outsider, reading this, would conclude that the citizens of this fair town are parochial, suspicious, elderly, overweight and very slightly mad. They would, however, not be entirely accurate. Reading a newspaper is a whole different kettle of fish from reading a novel, and the letters page in particular is a very odd fish indeed. For one thing, all papers have an agenda of one kind or another, depending on who their proprietors are. The Guardian, for example, is well-known for its left-wing, liberal-leaning views and opinions. The Daily Mail regards itself as the paper of sensible Middle England, although reading it actually resembles watching a barely tolerated uncle dying of an apoplexy. The Sun makes no apologies – it is smutty, chatty and up for a laugh, never truly serious about anything. Then you have to consider what kind of person would actually be so worked up about something that they feel the need to write to their paper. And remember, the nationals only print a selection of the printable each day. The need to write to a local paper in the hope of changing something: well, it generally smacks of a quiet, futile despair. No, in order to read a newspaper well, first one must negotiate the torrent of evasions, half-truths, exaggerations and downright lies that flood out of each page. In short, one must learn not only to read between the lines, but also to consider the significance of what is written. Hence my title: Reading is Hell.

Yes, I knew you thought I was going to start making fun of the town, but I'm doing that already, thank you very much. Rather, in this latest absurd interlude I wanted to think about the challenges that face the reader who wants to be honest and engage the text actively, rather than lazily letting the whole lot wash over one unchallenged. It is hard; to actively read requires a difficult leap of the imagination and mental courage. Most people passively accept what they are told or what stares up at them from the page. Such are literalists; all they see are the letters, words and phrases as is; they do not understand, because of the pedestrian way that they approach the task, that words have another life, a secret message behind their generally imputed meaning. The diligent, active reader, on the other hand, can infer greater levels of meaning by challenging what he or she reads. Religious books, such as the Torah , the Bible and the Koran, or Sufi tracts like Rumi's Mathnawi, actually tell the reader that the true value is not to be found in the words by themselves, but in their hidden import. The literalist cannot see this, however, and insists on the literal truth of what is written in his or her religious book of choice; such people become fundamentalists, and insist on wearing excessively large beards, or not wearing particular types of clothing, or generally not enjoying oneself. They call themselves religious and spiritual, but nothing could be further from the truth; they cling to a single, solid meaning of the word, and are then stuck in a narrow, moribund world of literal meanings where the spirit cannot soar. And thus they make reading Hell, because their limited perception of meaning makes it so.

The inquiring reader is very different. By understanding that a word can conjure up many possibilities; by knowing that phrases may have an idiomatic meaning as well as a literal one; by sensing that a story, such as a creation myth, is a tale to try and explain a circumstance rather than a description of something that actually happened; by asking questions back at the text, by challenging it to show its true shape, the diligent reader becomes enlightened and liberated. But to get to that plateau of freedom is difficult and harsh, as it means that one has to cast aside assumptions and expectations and read in a very different way. Not only that, but the journey can be a frightening one, once one realises that each and every written thing carries denotations and connotations, meanings coiled within meanings. In order to reach the light, once again reading must be Hell. And it can give one a terrible headache.

Let us take, as an example, one of the letters to the Reading Evening Post above. Remember, we have to evade the surface meaning and try to dig for what else there may be. Let us use the one titled 'Hunting Rage'. Firstly, notice the title. The writer herself will not have chosen this – instead, it must have been bestowed by a sub-editor. What is the sub-editor telling us here? Is he being neutral? Is he saying that hunters are angry? Or is he actually enraged by the fact of hunting? Now notice the letter itself. It consists of eight sentences and is organised as a single paragraph. The writer uses the first person singular pronoun eight times – a sign of insistence, or a symbol of an underlying lack of confidence? Does she actually represent the views of others, or does she merely hope so? Why is she so upset about the police doing their job, which at other times and circumstances she surely approves of? Why is she so upset? And why is she so afraid? As we ask the questions, an image comes to mind – that of an essentially lonely, insecure person who hides in a group and conceals her true feelings behind bluster and bombast. As you can see, careful reading unmasks the hand and the mind behind the text. Try it with this text; can you see me smiling between the lines? Remember, what you read is not necessarily what you should be reading; nor can you be sure if I am the voice of the author, or his puppet. Now let's get back to Dan and Taylor.

Nine: A drink in the Turks
And did those feet in ancient times walk upon England's pastures green?

William Blake, Jerusalem

In which Dan and Taylor manage to stagger up London Street and into the old coaching inn; They see something interesting; then they drink more, and the world begins to dissolve into metaphysical forms, or possibly drunken wooziness..

We crossed the bridge and the IDR, but not without some diversion. First off, another beggar came pelting hell for leather over the bridge, waving a can of Park Bench Special lager and shouting his head off. I thought he was coming at us first all, but he dashed past (with a helping shove from Taylor) and jumped into the pile of beggars we'd just gone by. Then he went thug on them, flailing with his fists and feet while they scattered. He was so angry that he seemed to be literally foaming at the mouth, and he was incoherent – just cursing and making enraged noises. We continued: On our right was the edifice of the Oracle, with the Kennet flowing sulkily through its centre. The IDR was a slow crawl of hot, tired, home-going traffic, heading from the flyover towards Queen's road. The metal walls of the shopping centre's car park bulged outwards, frozen grey sails gleaming dully in the dusty sunlight. We waited for the traffic lights to change, and watched three women, about twenty years old, across the other side of the road, bellowing their heads off – God knows why. They were loud enough to be heard above the sound of the traffic. Fuck, they could have stopped the traffic, they were so ugly. They were swigging from Bacardi Breezers and tagging the side of the Central Reading Youth Provision building, under the mural of black history. As we watched, though, a police car came hurtling westwards, lights and siren on, and they scattered. We finally managed to cross, then we went up the hill to the Turk's.

It was quiet at that time of day: Being July as well, the uni crowd weren't there. A couple were sitting on the bench outside, and within there were no more than ten or twelve, scattered around the deep sofas in the low-ceilinged front room, or playing pool at the back. I bought a pair of ales and some crisps, then we put our feet up on the sofa next to the fag machine. Another football match was playing on the telly in the corner, but no-one was watching it. From behind the table in front of the window came a deep, content snoring. A pair of feet were attached to it as well.

'I am starting to get very drunk, I believe', I said.

'Good. Crisps were a good idea, though – they'll soak it up a bit'.

Taylor ripped open a pack and started picking through them.

'Why can't pubs in this country do proper bar snacks? You have the choice of crisps or bags of peanuts, or, if they're really posh, bowls of peanuts on the bar which are covered in piss from people not washing their hands properly. It should be more like Spain – lots of tapas and stuff. I don't want to eat a full-metal dinner when I'm on the razzle, I'd rather snack.'

'Turkey's good for that, too – mezes and things. And raki. Have you tried that? Like arack, but smoother.'

Taylor frowned, trying to recall.

'Mm, yes, I did, when I was going through Cappadocia during a freezing cold winter. It was some restaurant, had a strange name….the SOS, that's it. We ate something delicious involving bits of lamb and chillis and rice from a big kind of wok, and drank raki. Bloody good stuff, as I recall. And the restaurant! At the end of a row of shops, all closed for the winter. There was mein host, who was working as boss, waiter and chef; While he cooked, he came out and in a frantic mix of Turkish, German, French and English, he'd tell us about the food and give us platters of bread and bottles of wine from his own vineyard. The place was kept warm by a huge wood-burning stove in the middle of the room, and there were those incongruous posters on the wall – you know, vast alpine scenes, crying gypsy children and boss-eyed kittens. The tables had cheap plastic cloths with a red and white check pattern and cigarette burns. The food was damn good.'

'I think I know the place – in Goreme, yeah? You know, the village in the middle of a valley of giant rock cocks which people used to live in? And the owner – round and bald with a big dark mustache, and chain-smoking.'

'That's the guy and the place, not that I got much of a chance to look around – I was back on the road the evening afterwards. When did you go there?'

'Not long after you and I went our separate ways. You know, I worked my way northwards until I hit the Black Sea, then I kind of followed it back round to the Marmara, then on to the Mediterranean.'

'We must have missed each other by a bit then, because I was there not long after we'd split up, too.'

I felt suddenly energised.

'Ah, man, that's incredible! We both end up at the same restaurant in the same village in the middle of nowhere – we probably just missed each other by a few days! That's some coincidence.'

'Well, it isn't really, not if you think of it; after all, we missed each other, and Goreme, despite its size, is a big tourist draw.'

'Just our luck then, that we didn't meet.'

'Hell, what does it matter now? Here we are, together again.'

We supped our beers.

'So, what did you think of it?' I asked.

'The place? Well, I didn't see giant rock cocks as you put it. Travelling through it was weird – a landscape of fists and fingers with caves dug into them. I walked up to this place with a big kind of castle literally dug out of this one great knarled hand of stone. From the top of it, you could see for miles, and the land looked like a dreadfully lined and wrinkled pair of hands.'

An image of the weird landscape of Cappadocia came to mind then – a place of deeply gouged valleys, seemingly arid but incredibly fertile, dominated by a volcano on the horizon.

'I still imagine it as Valley of the Phallus, though.'

'Well, perceptions alter from person to person, don't they? Let's take this place, Reading. How do you see it?'

I was slightly nonplussed by this.

'Um, well, it's home....my town. It's OK, I guess. Pretty boring, if anything. Reputation for being a bit rough in the evenings. Not the prettiest of places either.'

'Do you remember when we were in Cairo that time? How did you see that?'

I thought for a moment.

'Seething. Fascinating. Ancient. Crazy streets and mad traffic. Great food.'

'How would the average Cairene react to Reading, do you think?'

'OK, I see your point, Taylor – but they wouldn't find it interesting.'

'Maybe, maybe not. But they would look around, see an infrastructure that works, electricity and water that work all the time, and jobs and opportunities galore. And that's pretty much Heaven for some poor bastard from some of the places we've visited. It all depends how you see where you are, doesn't it? And that, Dan, is where you're having problems at the moment – you're in a trough, a bad pocket. Yet what you've shown me so far has been good, even if it has been limited to bar interiors.

'Try living here through the winter. Try to get an affordable house. Hell, Taylor, I lived better abroad.'

'Were you worried about housing then? Of course you weren't,' he said. 'So perhaps that circumstance has changed. If you don't like it so much, why are you here?'

I had absolutely no answer to that. I shrugged and carried on puffing on a cigarette. He carried on, saying something about the reason why he hadn't decided to come back. Good friend though he was, Taylor could also be incredibly annoying with his general, Zen calmness, something I'd forgotten. I half-listened to him, nodding as necessary, and looked round the bar. The pair of feet were still snoring happily; the couple from the bench walked in, arm in arm, gazing at each other; and there, in the corner by the fireplace, was the Fucking Weirdo from earlier on. He still had his nose in a notebook, but briefly glanced up and caught my eye. He grimaced, then went back to his perusal. I wondered whether he was actually following me, but decided that he probably wasn't. After all, I couldn't have been the only person at a loose end on a hot Friday afternoon in July in Reading, could I? I zoned back to what Taylor was saying.

'…but if and when I return for good, how I see what I'm doing will be important. Am I in a cage or out in the open? Free or stuck? You know what I mean, Dan, you've seen it as often as I have. People run away abroad under the illusion that it's somehow liberating, that they can escape all their problems. It just happens to turn out that what they're mostly trying to run away from is themselves. And that,' he gulped down his beer, 'is impossible. Oh, you can find yourself in an Ashram in Delhi, or up the side of an Andean mountain, sure, if you've been so bloody stupid as to lose yourself in the first place, but you can equally do it in, say, Milton Keynes. The location acts as a nice backdrop for the metaphysical adventure, that's what I'm saying.'

'Yeah, but I'd hardly have done what I've done if I'd stayed here, would I?'

'I wonder – for its size this place is remarkably cosmopolitan. No, the physical landscape is inextricably linked with what's going on in the soul. Perceive where you are as a dour, miserable, wet place, and you're likely to be dour, miserable and wet. But if you see that what is around you is exotic, mysterious and filled with peril and opportunity, then what happens to your perspectives? Reading can be every bit as exotic as, say, Bangkok; It depends where you're coming from.'

'If I hadn't been in Delhi when you were, we'd never have met.' Taylor picked up his glass and motioned to me to finish mine. He smiled.

'True, that was serendipitous. And it would have been a tragedy never to have met. But then, think about all those others you've never met and never will. Another one?'

He sauntered over to the bar and I mulled over what he was talking about. I got the gist of what he was saying, and realised that he was, in his own way, trying to buck me up. The truth was, I realised how much I'd missed his perspective, and how much I needed someone to bounce ideas, problems and worries off of. It was true; while I had a few other friends here, I'd effectively isolated myself for the last few months and become enveloped in my own introspective gloom, hating what I was doing, where I was, and even myself. Taylor had come like a little gleam of light showing through black clouds.

The snoring had stopped, and I saw the feet shift. A hand slowly appeared, reaching for the back of the bench. The fingers reached it, gripped, and hauled into view a vaguely-familiar, pale-faced man in his late fifties, with long strands of white hair and a few days' growth of grizzled grey beard. He propped himself so that I could see most of his head and torso, then rubbed his face vigorously, as if to scrub a stain off it. His clothes were deeply rumpled, covered in crisp crumbs and stained with God knows what. He caught sight of me, beamed and half-bellowed,

'Alright! Are ya winnin'?'

'Alright, mate. How are you yourself?'
'Not bad, not bad, all the better for me beauty sleep.' He gave a harsh, sour-breathed laugh that I could smell from where I was sat, then clambered up and staggered off towards the bogs. Taylor was coming back with a brace of pints; the man smiled and half-bowed as he went past.
'Christ, what is it with old blokes in this place? Don't they do anything but drink?' Taylor demanded when he sat down again. 'That one could have done with a bath or ten as well. Do you know him?'
'Don't think so, although something rings a bell.'
'I'll tell you, Dan, I didn't think I'd miss this country much while I was away, but ale is one thing I started craving after a while.'
'Yeah, that and curry. And beans. And Fish and Chips.'
'And Marmite.'
'All that stuff. I'd thought I'd gorge myself on it all when I got back.'
'But you didn't, because now you can have it whenever you want.'
'Well, Metaphysics are all fine and well, but they can't beat an empty stomach. Hunger proves what reality is.'
'Is the hunger real? And if so, is what you eat real?'
'Oh balls, Taylor – is our increasing drunkenness real? Is our booze real? Course it fucking is.' And I proceeded to demonstrate our current state of reality by taking a gulp, and therefore make us increasingly real in a world that was starting to look wobbly. The old guy, meanwhile, wobbled back to his bench, slopped another beer onto the table, and resumed his recumbent position.
'I still hold by what I said earlier. Where you are should have no effect on who you are, but it generally does. If you're down, try to look at your position in a different light.'
'Yeah, but you're also dragged down or pulled up by whoever you're with. You can be miserable anywhere, anytime when you're with the wrong person.'
'But isn't that my point? Now look at those two over there,' he said, gesturing to the couple with yet another cigarette, 'do you think they are looking at this bar in the same way and with the same attitude as us? Of course not; they have eyes for themselves and the place has become immaterial. Now let's

fast-forward a few years. They've been married a while, and intimacy has stripped them of illusions. They come here again; Do they see it as they did on this day? Again, no.'

'Well said, sir!', barked the man. He waved his glass at us, spilling some of the contents, then wiped his face again. 'Metaphysical disquisition in a pub, that's the stuff! And my kind of conversation, too.'

Taylor looked at him with a kind of weary amusement. 'So, are you real, or just a product of my over-worked imagination?' he enquired.

The man laughed his fetid laugh again. 'I may ask the same of you – I know I'm real, at least; And since I have been a regular here for more years than I'm too dishonest to admit to, while you seem to have magically appeared, as it were, I'm inclined to think it's you as is the spook.'

His mentioning that he was a regular made me suddenly realise who he was – Blake, the Turk's Head's resident alcoholic, who I hadn't seen for years. When I'd returned, I'd assumed he was dead, as it always seemed to be on the cards. It was well-known that his intention was to drink so much that, come his death, there'd be no need to embalm him, and he hoped his body would be allowed to be propped in a corner of the pub somewhere.

'It's Blakey isn't it?' I said. 'How's it going?'

'It's me indeed, sure as I'm sure of anything. Still in one piece. Still drinking. Heh!'

And he raised his glass once again.

I explained who Blake was, then Taylor said, 'So, do you live here then?'

'Explain 'here',' muttered Blake over his glass, before putting it down and belching loudly and looking pleased with himself.

'Whatever. This here's my bench anyhows. And you two? I don't believe I've ever had the pleasure before, but then I'm not so sure of anything, what with my brain mostly bein' on holiday with my liver.'

'Dan here's a local man. I'm travelling through; He's my host today.'

'What is it, a pub crawl or something of its ilk?'

'That's the way it's turning out,' I chipped in. 'We started off in Emmer Green and we're working our way round the town.'

Blake huffed. 'God, that's too much like hard work,' he said. 'Why move on, when you've got yourself nicely settled?' He turned to Taylor. 'And you say you're a traveller? Other countries and stuff, I suppose.'

'That's the measure of it, I guess,' grinned Taylor. 'Call it an extremely extended pub crawl'.

'Nah, you want to stay in one place. Why should I get up an go elsewheres? It all comes through here, eventually. What I can see with my imagination is enough, and sometimes more than enough. What I can't see, I got telly for.'

'But don't you want to go and actually see other places?'

'What for? You ever been to Spain?'

We both nodded. 'Well', he continued, 'I once went there. Torremolinos. That was back when I was married, way back in the seventies. Anyhow, I'd saved for ages for us to go. It wasn't like it is now – getting on a plane to Spain was like going to the Jungle in Africa must be like now. Anyhows, I'm saving and saving and all the time I'm thinking what it'll be like – you know, exotic food, paella and so on, and unknown drinks, guitars and flamenco and all. I was dreaming of it every night. And what happens when we finally get there? It's the bloody same as this place, but with more sunshine – fat blokes in vests drinking Watneys, egg and chips and bacon for breakfast, and your bloody neighbour in the apartment next to yours. And I hardly saw any Spanish, except for waiters. I was so disappointed that I came back and I've never gone back again. If I want an holiday now, all I do is pack the suitcases up here in me head, and I'm there. Bloody cheaper too!'

He drained his glass, then continued.

'Mind you, I heard what you said about how you see where you are – think I understood most of it. Now, I do like me beer, as perhaps you've noticed, and it, I think, makes the world a happier place. Many's the time, coming from here late at night, I swear I've seen angels sitting in the trees and on the rooftops, whispering and rustling their wings; That, and demons crawling from the sewers. Mind you, I've also seen a bin bag turn into a talking dog and back again.'

He sighed, looked into the depths of his glass and belched again, the look of enormous self-satisfaction crawling across his face once more.

'Anyhows, I think I need another doze. Nice to meet ya,' and so saying, he slipped down out of sight once more, and before long the contented snore resumed.

'If we don't get any food soon, we're going to end up like him,' commented Taylor. 'How about after we finish these we go and grab something quick to eat?'

'Fine by me,' I said. 'we'll head back towards town.'

We watched the football match for a bit, then lurched out of the door for the next part of the evening.

A diary entry

Another day. I'm itching to get going, to move, move, move, yet I can't. Feel like I'm stuck in a coffin with a fire inside, eating all my insides. I want to hand in my notice at work. I'm fed up with all the shit that Dave fucking Pullen keeps coming up with – today, he had me stuck in the archives all day – really boring. It's all really boring. The only good thing is that it's Friday – the weekend! Bad thing is, it'll soon be Monday again, and again work. I want to leave.

I'm seeing Jack again after I finish this and get myself ready. I don't know why. He's already put me through so much shit. After the bastard stood me up "cos I was playing football. Sorry babe" , I thought about dumping him, but what will I do? If he had even half an inkling of what he does to me….mmm. But he's still a bastard. My bastard. He's promised to be down at Bar Med, but I'm still going to phone him, make sure. At least Leticia and the girls are out and all, so I've got them as back up if it all goes pear-shaped. If he does "forget", that's it. I'll dump him, and see how he likes it. It's not as if there aren't other blokes around. Mark from Claims was eyeing me up today. He's pretty fit. Put it like this, I wouldn't kick him out of bed. Of course, Jack would get so bloody jealous if he caught me just eyeing up another bloke. Bloody men, why are they such kids? I thought they at least grew up a bit. Tonight I'm, going to wear THE red dress.! I'll give Jack a right eyeful…and if he doesn't turn up, I've half a mind to let someone else have a right eyefule.

Right, time to get ready. Wish me luck! X

Ten: Smoke and mirrors
We passed upon the stair, he spoke and wasn't there.
                    David Bowie, the man who sold the world
More Authorial interruption.
I knew the previous mini chapter would draw you in; that's why it's pasted there. There is something incredibly tempting and salacious about somebody else's diary, or private letter, some woman's bedroom musings; Why else was Richardson's Pamela such a hit when it first came out? Epistolary novels, or ones in the forms of a diary, are always going to be best-sellers; people are curious about that first-hand view, the way a character thinks and feels in a way that is alien to our own experience; we get the comfort of riding within another's mind, seeing the world through a different set of eyes, and the transformation of the mundane into the magical. This is what the average reader yearns for – a kind of escape. However, as Taylor so astutely noted earlier on, it is impossible to escape oneself – there can only be temporary refuge. Now, the novel is possibly a more wholesome and less expensive shelter than drink, drugs or moving abroad, but it is only ever a temporary respite from the mundane – eventually, we must all re-enter this world, that, by mutual acceptance, we call reality. The Author's job is to make this escape as satisfyingly 'real' as is possible, but any careful inquiry will reveal that even the best laid structure is immensely fallible. Now, here's me in my clown's cap, waving at you and reminding you that what you're reading is no more than a story. Take the first person narrative we've chosen for Dan, and compare it with the diary entry; When push comes to shove, which is really the most plausible? Honestly? The latter, of course, but even then, it's still fictive. For a first person narrative to be truly convincing, it would need to be:

    a) so full of action, sensation, flashes of insight, moments of introspection, lack of thought one moment, concentrated bursts, snatches of conversation heard and bits of this here, there and everywhere, plus frequent thoughts of sex if it is a male narrator and shoes if it is female, that it would be utterly impossible to follow a plot, or

    b)   Reduced. To short, snappy sentences. With little sketching in of what people said or did. Cut down to the bare minimum. Badly.

The fact of the matter is that life is not linear, it does not follow a story arc. The Author's task, as well as having a satisfactory plot structure, must also tease out a comprehensible storyline, a tenuous thread with a beginning, a middle and an end. This is difficult if you don't know where you're going. As a character in this creation, I absolve myself of all responsibilities for character and plot development – I'm just the spectator, jotting it down.
 Let's take another example of implausible story structure – Emily Bronte's Wuthering Heights. The whole thing is supreme contrivance from start to finish, and as a book, it should only be taught to those who already understand what a book should look like. For a start, it appears to consist of two immense diary entries, or letters, handily titled '1801' and '1802'. If they are diary entries, what else did Lockwood do for the rest of the year? '1801. Later. Went to the coaching inn and felt lonely.'? If they are letters, who to? Whatever they are, they show that the narrator, Lockwood, seems to be possessed of an almost supernatural memory for dialogues and situations, as does the narrator within the narrator, Nelly Dean. Not only that, but everyone can mimic Joseph in exactly the same way; observe Lockwood's copying of his speaking style, through to Nelly's (who, obviously, is Lockwood copying Nelly's copy of the original), and finally to Isabella's , which is Nelly, telling Lockwood some sixteen years after the event, copying Isabella's accent copying Joseph's, which in turn is Lockwood copying Nelly, as written by the real author, and is then interpreted by us. That's Joseph at five removes – ourselves, Bronte, Lockwood, Nelly, then Isabella – and still we keep a perfect copy of his bizarre accent? Then there is all the weird and coincidental stuff – the dog being strung up on a washing line, the visitation by Cathy's wraith, Nelly keeping a letter for twenty years, presumably always on her person, just in case some morose southern milksop gentleman comes to pay her a visit one winter. In spite of the absurdities of its structure, however, Wuthering Heights works, though God knows how: Given the distinctly (even for its time) old-fashioned structure, it still manages to entertain, keep the reader enthralled and the

Yorkshire moors full of Japanese tourists. Another example is the utterly ridiculous Dracula, which has to rank as one of the worst-written popular novels in history. Bram Stoker clearly just gives up on the individual diary structure halfway through, and has a single voice instead, even though it sounds exactly the same as Harker's, Van Helsing's and all the others. And the story is saturated with the author's character, worries, fears and obsessions. I personally regard it as almost unreadable, save for the fascination and fun to be had in delving into the writer's personality.

Dan doesn't strike me as being the most alert of characters, so how is it possible that he has managed to recall so much of his day with Taylor? It must be recall, after all; He's clearly telling a tale – we're not even experiencing this first hand. As such, it is all smoke and mirrors, but while you're enjoying it, who am I to complain?

Eleven: on the brink
Sumer is icomen in, lhude sing cuccu!
   William of Malmesbury, written in Reading Abbey ca. 1265
Our two heroes stagger back towards whence they came; They search out food; an encounter with the Oracle.

We came back down London Street. Taylor was alert, paying attention to all the houses and shops and businesses that lined it.

'So where next, Dan?'

'Well, let's just head back into town and grab something there, shall we? Needn't be much; just a burger or something, yeah?'

'Sounds OK to me...that's quite a funky little house..'

This was said about an old Tudor beamed cottage, twisted by age, just by a restaurant and an alleyway.

'What's down the alley?'

'Dunno. I've never been down there.'

'Shame on you, Dan – this is your stomping ground, and there are things you don't know about it? Come on.'

He led the way down it. Graffitti and tags were sprayed on the walls, and a few spliff butts lay scattered on the ground. It opened up into a small road with an old, regency-type building on the right and a more modern terrace of houses on the left. There was a church more or less directly ahead.

'What church is that?'

'I think it's St. Giles.'

We ambled towards it, Taylor taking in the spire, the building and its attendant graveyard.

'Now this I like – it's as if a bit of the countryside moved to town.' He frowned suddenly. 'Except...what the hell is that bloody stench?'

'Smells like Blakey's been having a party here with some of his less salubrious mates'.

It really was a gut-churningly foul smell, and I was probably right in my surmise. Closer inspection of the graveyard showed that it was littered in cider cans and bottles, cheap gut-rot whisky, food wrappers and splattered with vomit. The whole place had been mired by alkies. Someone had tagged one of the graves with the word 'Nestor'. What had appeared quite a pleasant

little churchyard was, in close-up, appalling. We hurried through the alley and came out on Southampton Street, where traffic, lighter as evening came on, chugged and flowed back down towards the IDR and the town centre. The air felt more humid and polluted than before, and more oppressive. Taylor leaned against the wall outside the church, and lit another cigarette.
'No need to hurry, is there? And this fag will get that horrible fetor out of the back of my throat.'
I sat down and lit up too. Taylor looked up Southampton Street, then back down towards the centre.
'Enlighten me,' he said. 'What am I looking at, and what direction am I squinting in?'
'That's the town centre more or less ahead of you, and you're facing north, or thereabouts,' I replied. 'There's the flyover for the IDR, the ring road we crossed on our way to the Turks. That ramp takes you on the northwards route, going towards Caversham and Emmer Green where we started. Straight ahead is the road towards St. Mary's Butts, and no jokes about arseholes please, it was where they used to practise archery. Just to the right is the Oracle..'
'Ah! We must visit her!' he muttered, and grinned.
'and beyond that is St. Mary's church,' I continued. Further on is Broad Street and Friar Street, then the station, from which it is possible to escape this bloody town.'
'You really must learn once more to stop being so pessimistic and negative, Dan. It doesn't suit you.'
'There are also lots and lots of pubs we haven't visited yet. I once calculated that if you tried to drink one beer in every pub within a few hundred yards of the station, there'd be a good chance you'd be dead of alcohol poisoning before you'd reach where we are now.'
'How many have we visited so far? Four, isn't it?'
'Yes. Plenty more ahead, though. Come on.'
And we carried on sauntering down the hill. As we came towards the roundabout, there was a great roar behind us, and an enormous old car, some ancient American monstrosity, appeared, belching a great plume of exhaust smoke. It pulled up at the traffic lights. It really was quite incredible, and really quite ridiculous. It was painted black, with red and orange flames along the wings; it had white-walled tyres, but not real ones –

instead someone had painstakingly painted them, but done an awful job. There was plenty of chrome and tailfins and the thing's hood was down. The trouble was, it was all out of proportion, as though someone had tried to nail two completely different cars together. Most absurd of all was the little man driving. He was in full early-rocker uniform, which was too big for him, and complete with jet black Elvis-style quiff and DA. He looked awfully pleased with himself. He flicked a cigarette into his mouth, or rather tried to, as it hit the side of his face instead. He bent down to retrieve it, then sat back up, this time with the hair having slid sideways over his bald pate. I burst out laughing at this sight, as did Taylor. This obviously pissed off Bald Elvis terribly, because he tried to roar away from the lights in a haze of tyre smoke; Instead, he bunny-hopped the car and stalled, making us laugh even more as we crossed the road in front of him. Doubled up, we entered the Oracle by the car park entrance and found ourselves by one of the bridges. There were traffic cones across it, and a horsey-looking man directing people away. On the bridge were men with large nets, and in the water were a couple of really bad-tempered looking swans. Other men were on the bank, also with nets and long poles.

'sorry, if you could just go that way please, that's right, thank you,' said the equine-faced man to a woman, then to us, 'and where are you going?'

'We just wanted to pass through,' I said. 'What's going on here?'

'It's these bloody swans,' answered the man, 'they've turned into a right pair of nuisances, pestering people for bread and so on. It's gone too far today now. They attacked a little kid for her sandwich and drew blood, so we've got to move them on, but they're being a right pain in the arse to catch. If you want to go into the centre, please use the other bridge.'

We walked by the bank, and watched the somewhat chaotic attempts to catch the errant swans. This involved one man with a pole poking the thing hopelessly at the swan , while another tried to catch the animal in his net. This only served to piss the swans off even more, as they fluttered and splashed around and generally evaded the capture attempts, much to the merriment of the gathering crowds on the banks. We walked up to the mutiplex, then crossed over on the footbridge.

'Right, where shall we eat?' asked Taylor, as we passed the various restaurants and diners on this side of the Oracle.
'Let's just grab a burger,' I said.
'Fine by me.'
So we went into Macdonald's and ate their sad excuses for food, along with dozens of others enjoying their fare. Well, they must have been enjoying it, as they weren't evincing any signs of disgust, like vomiting. Once we'd finished, we went into the Shopping centre itself and up the escalator. I pointed out the now-empty information booth.
'There's your Pythian oracle, Taylor – looks like she's buggered off.'
'Never mind. Let's get out of here ourselves. I hate these places at the best of times, but they get creepy in the evening.'
A few wan faces passed through, and a few groups of party goers. Here and there were people gazing into the now-closed shops, hungry for the clothes and goods on display.
'It's like some vestibule for ghosts, isn't it? Look at them, drifting along into oblivion.'
'This is Reading. It's a commercial town. Take away the opportunity for commerce, and the inhabitants feel lost. It's why, for example, there are hardly any old buildings – there's always been new money coming in, and new money always wants new buildings. The attitude of the typical Readingensian is 'What's in it for me?''
'A commendable attitude for the literal-minded capitalist.'
'Everyone wants cash, but that's about it,' I continued as we came outside and crossed Holy Brook before it plunged back under the ground, 'Look around at all the flash cars and new flats. It's all image, and all built on tick. Come a financial crisis, and most of these buggers'll be joining the beggars.'
'You're hard on them, which suggests you're being hard on yourself – who knows exactly what they want? Chances are it's a nice house and a decent wage and the chance to be a bit happy. Don't blame a cannibal for living in a cannibal culture – it's all he's known, so of course he's going to act like a cannibal.'
'I guess you're right,' I said as we walked up Chain Street, past Heelas, now renamed John Lewis, and St Mary Minster.
'Where are we headed, anyway?' asked Taylor.

'I thought Friar street, then we'll head up that and round again. A cheap beer in a Weatherspoon's, anyway.'

We walked across Broad Street and into Union Street, known to one and all as Smelly Alley, due to it once having been where all the butcher's shops and fishmongers were situated. Only one fishmonger and one butcher remained now, everything else having been taken over by an eclectic mix of different businesses. There was still a faint tang of fish in the air despite the shop having closed a couple of hours before, adding to the clammy and uncomfortable evening air. Stepping over a few stray pieces of old vegetable from the greengrocer's that had been left to rot in the middle of the alleyway, we came out onto Friar street. Standing on the opposite pavement was Elvis, done up to the eyes in his usual finery, namely a yellow Elvis Tshirt, blue Elvis jeans, an Elvis belt and blue shoes with a picture of Elvis on. Being a hot day, he didn't have his red satin Elvis jacket on. He was a rather weedy guy with buck teeth and a very greasy quiff. No one knew what his real name was; he was always just known as Elvis, and had been ever since I was young. He rolled goofily and happily along the road, listening to some soundtrack inside his head. A few cars and buses cruised lazily down the road, weary from the day's heat; small groups wandered languidly, aiming for the various bars here and there. A thought struck me.

' How much have we actually drunk?'

'How many had you had before I walked in the door at the White Horse?'

'I'd just started on my second.'

'Let's see… there was that pub on the way down, we had a bottle each there, then the place with the two philosophers in, one there, after that, two in the Hobgoblin and two in the Turk's. That's eight for you and seven for me.'

'So why aren't I feeling as pissed as I should?'

'Probably because it's coming towards eight o'clock and it's hot.'

'Probably. Another one?'

'Why not?'

And so we walked into the Hope Tap.

An Advert

Managers are born, not made.
Join the country's fastest growing pub chain as a manager and prove you've got what it takes.
We have openings NOW for the right kind of person.
You are dynamic, ambitious, personable and waiting for the right opportunity. We are looking for someone like you.
Have you got what it takes to work in an ever-changing, fast-paced working environment? Could you handle a team of up to ten staff and deal with the demands of the modern-day licensed victualling trade? Would you be able to hand the requirements of a thriving business that deals with members of the public each day, every day? A business with YOUR name over the door? If the answer's yes, then apply now. You are the kind of person we are after. Join our management trainee scheme, and you could be in charge of a pub within two years. In return, we offer a competitive salary plus benefits. Wages start at £18,000 (pro rata) and performance bonuses.
Come and join our family.

That's what it said, so it did, right up until I heaved me load over it, sure.

Twelve: Cheating bastards
Bought my first real six string, at the local five and dime,
Played until my fingers bled, twas the summer of sixty nine
Bryan Adams
The Author sticks his oar in yet again; He offers further unwelcome pontification; he wonders exactly where he's going and how he will contrive to get his characters into the desired place for the next section.

Alright, I own up. You've got me fair and square. I put my hands up and confess, guv'nor. You've got me bang to rights, and all those other tiresome clichés. As it must be glaringly obvious to even the dimmest of my readers, I have totally stolen my story from the embrace of another. In short, it is as Socrates bellowed earlier – this tale is no more than Dante's Inferno applied to two blokes on a pub crawl. It's painfully obvious really, isn't it? Dan Thompson, or Dan T.; the use of a dead poet, in this case Samuel Taylor Coleridge, shorn of his first name, spouting metaphysics, and made to be a pretty cool dude; Taylor's command to Dan at the beginning to follow him in order to sort his life out; their descent into Reading and beer after beer. You've got to admit, though, it's all pretty clever – I've tried to keep various analogies going, and our two heroes are following an admittedly rough clockwise spiral. If you don't believe me, go back and check – see? Good, isn't it? Eh? Eh? Even Beatrice, or Beattie, gets a look in. But now I'm a bit stuck – they've deviated somewhat, and I'm in a quandary as to do to put them back on the right track next. But more of that later.
 Yes, yes, I know you're probably all quite upset; I can see you rendering my book unto the floor, shouting in disgust and then taking this back to your local bookseller, demanding a refund for having been mislead, or possibly turning away in horror from the page in front of you, but please, BEAR WITH ME. Let me explain. The fact is, most writers are so lazy that they can't be bothered to invent a plot – instead, they just crib from someone else, or bodge two different tales together. Why else do you think there are only seven different story archetypes globally? It's because no-one can be arsed inventing new ones. Now this

particular tale is essentially the 'wandering hero, discovers wisdom/ secret of fire/ eternal life/ a sticky end at the end of his travels, returns home with it (or not, in the case of the sticky end scenario, in which he might come back in a box. Or a bag)' type thing. Simple as that. Do you think Dante had the copyright on that? Of course not. He nicked his idea off someone else, and added a bit of orthodox catholic Christian imagery to it. What he did do, though, is work out an intricate scheme, plot and timeline before he got down to the weary, dirty business of scrawling. Since I don't have the luxury of that, my task being to describe a whole day as quickly as possible, I have taken the liberty of, ahem, liberating his plot and butchering it as I see fit.
And why not do it? Everybody does. It's even given literary gravitas in the Islamic world in the form of something called the *nazire*, which is essentially a courtly poem that rips off the theme of another. Books generally refer back to other books, tales, legends and myths. They may claim originality, but the vigilant reader, which I hope you are becoming (indeed, you must have seen the Dante thing way before now), by judicious flaying of the story's skin and paring its muscle down, will easily discern the bones of a far more ancient legend lying underneath, just as surely as being able to track down the author's mind, as I have mentioned before. All I'm doing is making it easier for you here. I hope you don't mind. This tale is, in short, a bad parody of a Christian story, allegory and vision of Hell. This, by the way, is no time to comment on the real Dante's apparent profligacy when it came to bedding anything with an orifice. Rather, we could comment on the imagery of the Pilgrim and Dan. Are they in any way similar? So far, no: Dan does not appear to react to the various situations he finds himself in, nor does he appear to grow in realisation. Then again, his tendency not to really notice what's going on around him has been commented upon. All he grows is increasingly drunk. Likewise, Taylor doesn't seem to do much but chunk out metaphysical musings. So he's exactly like Virgil, then. As to the story: why is it being written? Why is it a parody of a Christian Fable? I've already provided an answer, but as the Author, you know that I am possibly unreliable; perhaps there's another reason. If so, it's up to you to dig it out, and good luck to you.

To return to my point about books talking about other books, here's an image for you.

There's a type of party game that's tremendous fun to play when everyone's drunk. You get everyone in a circle, each person facing the back of the person in front, and holding them by the shoulder at arm's length. At a given signal, everyone sits; Lo and behold, they are sitting on each others' laps. Each person supports the weight of someone else without being crushed. You are then supposed to waggle one foot and a hand in the air and go 'wooo!', but this is optional. Don't try it with both feet. Anyway, this is the image I have of books and tales and authors; a great ring of people supporting each other, whispering into the ear of the one in front.

They're not waving a foot in the air and going 'wooo!' though. Except for Charles Dickens.

Now what am I going to do with the two heroes? At the moment, they are beginning to stray. It is, as Taylor pointed out, nearly eight, and they have another six hours of drinking ahead of them. If we are to follow the Dantean plan, they should now be entering the equivalent of the wood of suicides and profligates in the seventh circle. Yet I can't see it happening. In fact, the whole Dante theme was quite accidental at first, but has solidified as I've written – now it threatens to break down once more. Well, let's see where it goes. After all, I'm just as at the whim and mercy of the tale as the characters and you, of course.

Thirteen: Dead souls.
Blah Blah Blah.

Iggy Pop et al

An amazing intervention; everything is scuppered and suddenly all bets are off.

There was a whiff of stale carpet, cigarettes and spilled ale as we opened the door into the Hope Tap; In the corner by the entrance were the Terrible Drunks, a group of old and pissed up Irish blokes, singing contrived songs about the good old land; one of them was looking dazedly at a poster for something or other that seemed to be covered in puke. The rest of the clientele was a mix of different types – students, office workers who hadn't managed to get home, separate groups of young men and women starting their evening out. Also at the bar was The Fucking Weirdo, and he was staring directly at us.
'Look, Taylor, it's him again! The weirdo from the bus – I'm sure he's following us. He was in the Turks earlier on as well.'
'Are you absolutely sure? It could just be coincidence.'
'No, I'm sure – I'm going to have it out with him.'
But before I could approach him, he came up to us, waving his hands like an idiot.
'No, no, no! You shouldn't be here!', he shouted in desperation. Taylor looked as surprised as I did.
'Why the fuck not, and who are you to tell me where I should be?' He demanded.
'Sorry, sorry, but you shouldn't be here, isn't it obvious?' he pleaded, obviously in some kind of distress.
'What the hell are you going on about?' I asked, holding down a sudden urge to laugh at his forlorn appearance. He came closer, and whispered,
'Hell is exactly what I am talking about. That is where you are.'
Taylor and I both said 'What?' and laughed, as did a few people at the bar who'd been eavesdropping.
'You are in Hell!' he insisted, 'or rather you would be if you'd taken the right direction.'
I could only gape in amazement at this bloke.
'What are you on, and where can I get some?' Taylor asked.

Listen to me - please listen,' he said, gripping my arms. 'You are not where you should be – the plan, you have to follow the plan – look!'

He let me go, suddenly scrambled in his pocket, and brought out a tattered paperback, filled with strips of envelope, torn-out bits of notebook, and diary pages. I swear there was also a used cotton-bud. He also produced his notebook and a rough kind of map, showing something circular. I wasn't sure whether to laugh at him, pity him or punch him one. The barman looked over at us, unsure as to what to do.

'It's very simple, don't you see? You – you are Dante. And you, Mr. Taylor Coleridge, are the Virgilian figure, guiding your charge towards a greater sense of self-awareness. You..'

Taylor suddenly erupted in fury, something I'd never seen him do.

'You cheeky, mad little fucker, you have been following us! What's your bloody game, you weirdo? Who are you?'

The figure drew himself up in a ridiculous show of pride.

'I am the Author. You are my characters, and you will return to the plot laid out for you!'

We both burst out laughing at this. Someone piped up, 'and if they're characters, I take it I'm one and all?'

'No,' replied the Fucking Weirdo Author, 'You are irrelevant, because you are one of the Damned in my story. I mean, you are just a metaphor, or analogy.'

This elicited, 'I'll analogy you, twat features!', and things would probably have got ugly if one of the bar staff hadn't come round the bar and gripped the Author by the arms.

'Right you, out! I don't want another word, and I won't have you upsetting my customers, come on with you!'

There was a smattering of applause from the Terrible Drunks, to which the barman replied, 'Carry on and I'll have you buggers out and all!'

The Author was still trying to shout to us.

'No! You must return! You should be in – in circle seven, ring two - the Dolorous Wood with the Suicides and the Profligates! Turn back right! Turn Right! Keep turning right! I'll be waiting!'

And the door closed on him.

'Bugger me!', I said.

'Not right now,' replied Taylor, 'I could do with a drink first.'

'Do you think he will be waiting? If he is, I'll fucking deck him!'
'Nah, he wouldn't be that stupid, to show his face to us again.'
We got our drinks, accompanied by some staring from a few punters and an apology from the barman, and found a corner of the beer garden that wasn't too sticky. It was a beautiful, but humid, evening now. Dusk was drawing on, and the garden was already pretty much in shadow. Taylor and I sat in silence for a while, smoking yet another fag and, I suspect, sharing the same thoughts.
'Do you have any idea at all as to what that was all about?' I asked.
'Nothing. I really don't know,' replied Taylor. 'You were right though – he was following us. Maybe just you. Have you ever seen him before today?'
'Never.'
'Perhaps he fancies you.'
'Ha ha. Could just as easily be you. How did he know your name, anyway?'
'That's not so difficult – he must have overheard me in, what was it, er, the Blagrave?'
'True, but wouldn't we have seen him?'
'Might have been sat down with his back to us or something.'
I mulled it over.
'He seemed very worked up about us being in here- and what was that about Hell? What was he going on about?'
Taylor smiled.
'Now I'm sure of it. He must have been in the Blagrave when Socrates and Plato came out with that crack about Dante. You said earlier about how he had his nose in a book; Odds on it's a copy of Inferno. His feverish little imagination's got the better of him, and now he's convinced that we're some pair of allegorical figures.'
'Yeah, I guess you're right. And anyway, it's not as if any of that stuff in Dante has happened to us.'
'Have you read the Divine Comedy?'
'Me? Well, I know of it, of course. Can't say I've read it per se. Why?'
'Nothing. Well, maybe something: I'm just mulling something over.'
'What?'

'Me. Taylor Coleridge, name of a poet. You, Dan Thompson, or Dan T. You, in your mid-thirties – about the same age as the fictional Dante in his poem, at a crossroads in your life, wondering where to go. I show up, we go on a journey – and did you notice the word 'Hell' on the bus stop? And we went downhill from there! And we met two guys named Socrates and Plato – hmmm.'

Taylor stopped, lost in amused thought. He was obviously thinking things through.

'I don't really know the story myself, but I can understand where the guy was getting off. That's why he yelled about turning right – if I recall properly, Dante and Virgil keep turning in a clockwise spiral.'

He got his cigarette packet out, tore the back off it, and put the piece of card on the table.

'Shame we don't have a map,' he muttered. 'You got a pen? Cheers. Now help me here...where did we start off?'

Over the next half hour or so, we tried to work out exactly where we'd been so far, and draw a map in proportion. We wrote down what we'd drunk, who we'd seen and, as far as possible, the topic of conversation. I drew a rough map of the streets of central Reading, and continued onto a few beer mats to show where Emmer Green was. The end result was not so much a clockwise circle as a wobbly straight line, coming down from Emmer Green, into Caversham, then over the bridge and so on. It did, however, show a tendency to move to the right. Taylor racked his brains for what parts of the story he knew, and sketched in the words 'Limbo' over the Blagrave, and the words 'Styx?', 'Acheron?' and 'Phlegethon?' over the rivers Thames and Kennet.

Lastly, in Friar Street, he wrote 'Wood of the Suicides – where?'

'That's what he said, wasn't it? Something about turning right, and we should be in circle seven.'

'That's right – but was he?'

I admit, I was starting to get a bit freaked by the whole thing – blame the amount of booze I'd already had, and being stalked by some weirdo. Taylor laughed.

'Of course he's wrong – just a rather sad bloke who got a mad idea lodged in his head. However, this is quite cool, don't you think? He's suggested that our trip tonight is somehow pre-

ordained and planned. He's also opened up a set of metaphysical doors, as it were, and made us characters in some kind of re-telling of Dante's story. Think of it like we're in a kind of labyrinth – one with no walls and dead ends as such, except the ones that are part of the real, physical town. All the dead ends are in our heads. I just wish I knew the story more.'
'Why, so we could follow it?'
'Maybe, maybe not – in a way, it would be fun to find out. Equally, it would be fun not to follow his crazy set of rules and see if he turns up again, waving his hands and his map. Then you could deck him. Let's face it, it could make the whole evening far more entertaining.'
' So what do you reckon then?'
'Well, let's finish these, then turn right and see where we end up next.'
As he said, we didn't have anything to do apart from get drunk, and as it didn't really matter where we did this, we could go where we liked; why not play along for ourselves and see what happened? We went up to the bogs before moving on. Washing our hands, we looked out of the windows down on to Friar Street. Sainsbury's was just closing up and the last few staff were locking the doors behind them; A few people were waiting for buses heading towards Caversham; And small knots of revellers wandered along, shouting. One group were dressed as cavemen and women. Taylor watched the scene attentively.
'Is Reading always like this?'
'Every Friday and Saturday night, yes,' I said. 'It has a reputation for high weirdness. Even hardened Londoners who come here by accident tend to just shake their heads in disbelief.'
 Coming down the stairs, we passed a woman in her twenties labouring up, and extremely drunk. She winked at us as she passed, and put her fingers to her lips.
'Sh-shh,' she said, 'Say nuffink. I ain't here, right?' Then she tip-toed the rest of the way up, stopping only to say 'Sh-shh!' to her reflection, then giggling.
'Time for some fresh air,' said Taylor, and we pushed through the now-heaving bar into the hot evening street.
'Right then, left or right?' I said.
'Let's follow the game,' said Taylor. 'To the Right!'
'To the seventh circle!'

'To the wood of suicides, whatever that is!'
'Just wish I knew where that was.'
And we turned right.

Fourteen: I am not who you think I am
...idle men and the like, who seek stories and fairy tales...
                                                                Rumi

The Author is distinctly upset; He bewails ingratitude and discourses upon the fictive and the real.

Or not, as the case may be; I have said I am unreliable, and so I have shown. The summary has very little to do with this interlude. In no other way have I shown my unreliability than in my sudden appearance as a character at the front of the stage, as it were. Now, you may think that that was a highly odd thing to do, and perhaps you are right, but think on a bit more, dear reader: I have already expressly and frequently said that this is a mere fiction; that it is mine, and mine to do with as I will; and that I can and will appear in it. Now think on – what purpose does my intervention have upon the two characters? Suddenly, they have a purpose of sorts; not only that, but they are aware of it. They have also expressed ignorance of certain facts – they don't know much about the journey sketched out in Inferno. In fact, if you go back to when they were crossing Reading Bridge this afternoon, you may have noticed Taylor's comment about the Thames and its being perceived as the river Styx. Of course, being perfectly accurate, the river Acheron should have been mentioned here to follow the allusion to Dante. However, this all goes to show that the characters are perfectly fallible in what they do and say; They get facts wrong, as we all do; they exaggerate, over-elaborate, and lie, as we all do; in fact, the infallible character is untrustworthy, and that goes for the Author as well – it is an act of dishonesty. Now, consider this: By thrusting myself so firmly into the spotlight, I have conclusively shown my nature as a fictional creature, and a sorry sight I cut as well, it must be said. As such, it therefore follows that a) I cannot be the author and b) Dan's first-person account is also fictive and therefore unreliable. It then raises the next uncomfortable idea: If you can't trust me, being fictional, then who? Not only that, the characters are now aware of the story arc, albeit dimly; What does that imply? As to my identity, all I can say is, I Am Not Who You Think I Am.

For a start, no matter how much I would love to be (and who wouldn't?) I am not the Omnipotent, Omniscient God of this particular microuniverse that happens to be this story. As I explained at the beginning, I don't have a clue as to what is going to happen next. Your guess is as good as mine, although if you have a spare copy of Inferno to hand you might find it useful. Very well, then, am I the Story itself, desiring to be written, wishing only to view its own outcome? Possibly, but that still does not account for the fact that I am being written by someone. It may be that Stories exist within the mind; However, they have no real strength or influence until they are shared, passed on, written down – that is when the Story of the Wandering Prince, or the Third Son, or the Discoverer of Her True Destiny, takes on power and is disseminated across a thousand different cultures.

No, I am the author, but just as I appear in one way on these pages, so I have another existence outside of it. Consider this, though – in these interludes, I often appear as something of a smug smartarse, showing off what I already know and indicating what may occur next. In the story itself, I am not much to write home about, am I? Now look at yourself, dear reader. Go on, go to the mirror, and take a damn good look at yourself. What do you see? How do you read the book of the self? I'll wager you don't read it the same as someone else. It's like the difference between someone sitting down into their favourite armchair to read a favourite, well-read tome, and someone picking up the same book, but this time it's unfamiliar to them. It's alien territory, to be scrutinised or ignored as the reader sees fit. And just as a book has many pages, so you show a different page to your reader according to how you see fit. Imagine a party full of people who know you: They may all have different opinions of you, simply because they have seen differing pages of the book that is your soul. So please, dear reader, do not presume to judge me on the paltry few leaves of myself I have so far displayed. To read the entire story of someone else, it is necessary to become that other person in their entirety, from beginning to end – is this possible? I would suggest it is not: In which case, each person, apart from, possibly, ourselves, is essentially unknowable. Do not, I beg of you, place me in a pigeonhole; I flatly refuse to conform. Accept only this: that I am having fun doing this as I write, and I hope I have set you an interesting maze of ideas in which to play. Of course it is limited: haven't I just said I am fallible?

Fifteen: Back on track?
History is a nightmare from which I am trying to awaken.
                                                              James Joyce
In which our drinking buddies try to negotiate their ways through a Reading that has suddenly become a more sinister place, both bereft of and gravid with meaning and connotation; they saunter into the next watering hole, wondering if they have arrived at the correct place; they encounter more high weirdness.

You could tell that evening was drawing on apace – more and more the streets were drained of normal people and being replaced with either the drunk, the weird or the weirdly drunk. A pack of twenty-something lads, in tight casual trousers and shirts, came blaring and charging past, heading towards Jongleurs; in their wake was another hen party, this time all done up in Bunny Girl costumes, aiming for the same place; a tramp was pushing along his dilapidated Asda trolley, stopping at each bin in search of either food or particularly interesting specimens of the day's flotsam, which he would add to his mobile mound. We strolled past Smelly Alley and its fishy reek again, casually observing the unrolling scene of incipient riotous partying.
'Where do you reckon The Wood Of Suicides would be, anyway?' , I asked.
'Not sure – according to Weirdo, it's probably along here, somewhere. Let's think – looks to me like we're headed towards somewhere pretty lively – does that sound like a suicide-prone place to you?'
'Only if you're a Billy No-Mates.'
'There must be somewhere along here that is filled with an empty, bereft, lonely atmosphere, somewhere you'd rather die than own up to drinking in...'
'Taylor, I think the answer's just ahead of us.'

There was the picture of a military man in a solar topee, blowing upon his wind instrument; A neglected, sorrowful bar on a corner:
'The Bugle. This must be it.'
We went in through the low door into the low-ceilinged room of a bar that had died about twenty years previously. There were a few locals inside, who were instantly hushed by the presence of strangers in their midst. The carpet was mostly held together by spilt beer, fag ash, and most probably sputum. The atmosphere within had probably not been changed since the previous year. It was a ghostly, rancid, unloved hole. A middle-aged bar woman with a bubble perm and large glasses stopped wiping pint mugs and composed herself in front of us, one hand on an ale pump, and her face frozen in a semi-welcoming, semi-threatening rictus.
'Good evening, what can I get you?'
This was, I noticed, the first time all day that any one in a bar had actually asked me what I wanted rather than wait to be told.
'Two pints of best, thanks.'
'We don't have any.'
'No bitter at all?'
'None.'
'OK then, two pints of lager?'
'Sorry.'
'What have you got?'
'Cider or gin.'
'Nothing else?'
'No. We're having problems with the suppliers. If you don't want those, you'll have to go elsewhere.'
'No problem, we'll have two ciders.'
'Do you want ice in that?'
'Er, no, I think we can live without it, thanks.'
'That's just as well,' she said, 'as we don't have any ice either.'
I gave her the money, which she took with a vehemence that surprised me, then slammed the change on the bar. Taylor and I took the corner seats near the window, facing onto the street. A very large man with a dark beard and a mullet haircut stared down at us, silently threatening us to challenge him over what was indisputably a pint of bitter in his large mitt.

'No doubt we're in the right place,' I muttered to Taylor.
'It would appear so.'
'What next?'
'I don't know. I don't think we're meant to do anything. If something's supposed to happen, it just will.'
'Then how the hell do we know that we're doing whatever it is that we're supposed to be doing. Fuck it, Taylor, this is bollocks!'
'Yes, but interesting bollocks, don't you think?'
'No, it's bloody not! I don't mind doing the pub crawl thing, but I never expected, in my whole lifetime, that I'd end up in the sodding Bugle!'
The large man at the bar growled. I mean, he actually growled, like a large dog or bear. He obviously didn't like me denigrating his favourite watering hole.
'The point is,' I continued, somewhat more quietly, 'there are more salubrious places to go than this. Is there any point in following round some mad whim? It's not as if we really know the story, anyway. C'mon, let's neck these and go somewhere better, eh?'
Taylor was only half-listening to me. He had his fingers to his temple and was trying to squeeze a thought out.
'From what I recall, don't Dante and Virgil end up at the very centre of Hell, on a frozen lake where all feelings die? Where do you reckon that could be?'
'Oh, Christ knows! Anyway, it's sodding July! And Reading is not noted for its ice-skating facilities! Come on, let's go!'
'Yes, Go!' roared the large man. 'Get out of my pub, since ye find it so offensive!'
He lowered his pint and lurched over towards us.
'We don't like newcomers here.'
'That's right,' piped up someone else. 'Piss off.'
'So why don't you drink your drinks, RIGHT NOW, and get out of here. Leave us be.'
The barmaid said nothing, but judging from her stance and the look on her face, she was about to order us out anyway. I took a quick swig of the cider, then decided to forget it.
'Come on Taylor, this isn't it.'
'I'm inclined to agree with you,' he said. 'Good evening.'
So we beat a hasty retreat from there.

Back on the street, all of a few minutes after we'd left it, there was still the steady stream of incoming revellers. There was also the Weirdo, across the road from us, looking very pleased with himself, and jotting something in his notebook. He caught sight of me and legged it down towards the junction of Friar Street and Station Road before I lost sight of him behind a crowd of people.

'I saw the bugger again!' I said.

'Me too,' replied Taylor. 'He was looking very content – do you reckon we were in the right place for his mad little scheme?'

'But nothing happened!'

'Perhaps it wasn't meant to.'

'Ah shit, Taylor, I can't handle this crap. Can't we just go back to discussing my miserable life?'

And I was feeling miserable as well. On top of the alcohol, on top of Taylor's 'metaphysical disquisitions', I was now trying to deal with what the Weirdo had said, and it was doing my head in. We came to the junction, filled with bustling crowds of all sorts of people, some dressed in weekend finery, others more mundane, and some in strange, canivalesque get-ups. The splendid Victorian baroque brickwork of the shops and offices that lined Victoria Street was lit up, something that Taylor pointed to, fascinated by the extravagant amount of work that had gone into it. Suddenly, rock-solid, red-brick, dumb old Reading had become something else, something I didn't quite understand. Taylor was game for traversing this strange maze; after all, not having been here before, it was all new for him – what the place was, and what the place meant, were one and the same thing. As for me, it was my home town, and that meant tedium, boredom, sameness, mundanity. But now it was as if it was trying to escape that set of definitions and become something rare and strange, as exotic as a far-flung desert city, a fabled Samarkand. Either it was changing as I moved through it, or I was being transformed under the influence of Taylor and the Weirdo. These were the thoughts going through my head, I swear: I tried to express this to him, but all I could say right then was,

'My head is feeling fucking weird. I think we need a proper drink.'

'Lead on – I follow your bidding.'

'Let's try the 3 B's - it should be clear of pensioners by now.'
We walked towards the town hall, another confection of whimsy in brick, past the glut of bars at the end of Friar Street with their slowly increasing queues and shaven-headed bouncers. The sound of music from the various places was gradually increasing, a series of heavy thudding beats that contested with each other for dominance of the street in a grand cacophony that underscored the shouting, yelling, laughing and yelping of the partygoers. From the town hall itself came the noise of a band, along with cheering and applause.
'They must have a live set on tonight.'
'Let's see.'
There were a couple of bouncers on the door, but it was a free event – according to the poster on the wrought-metal gates, a 'blues and boogie night'. We went through, and were immediately hit by the heat – a terrible, humid fug, composed of sweat vapour, beer, and copious cigarette smoke. The place was absolutely heaving. In the tiny stage area next to the front windows, a blues and rock combo were thumping away, and their lead singer, an early middle-aged woman in a tight leather dress and wild, straw-blonde hair was blasting out a version of a Meatloaf song. We squeezed our way through the crowd to the bar. Everybody was clearly feeling the heat; people were waving their hands in front of their faces to try and cool down, or tugging at their clothing. Next to us, three guys were having an animated and very noisy discussion as they waited to be served.
'Yeah, well, fuck God,' said one of them, a lanky boy of about eighteen. He puffed at his fag, and brushed some ash off his clothes. 'It's not as if he exists, anyway.'
'You wouldn't say that if He struck you dead, would you?' said another. 'It'd be the other way round!'
'Yeah, like fuck,' lanky snarled. 'Look. Come on, God, here I am, take your best shot! Twat! See? Nothing.'
' I bloody hate God-botherers,' said the third kid, a short, dark-haired and spotty specimen. 'We had some of those Jehovah's witnesses, or something like that, banging at the door the other day. You'll like this – They're giving me all the old chat about being saved and joining them and all that shit, then they ask me if I believe in Jesus. You know what I told them? I told them 'I believe that Jesus and Peter were fucking bumchums'. That shut

the fuckers up. Then I start telling them how I'm a Satanist and I'm cooking a couple of babies at the moment, and would they like to come in for the orgy? And so on, till they fucked off.' He looked on triumphantly as his mates hooted with laughter.

'That told 'em Chas,' said the second character. 'Ere, Bri, what do you do if you get any coming round?'

The lanky one said, 'I feel like punching the fuckers, but I'd tell you what I'd love to do – this'd be funny – have a pair of devil's horns, you know, the type they sell at Halloween – and a pitchfork ready by the door, then when they come, I'd put them on, open it and say,' and here he put on a deep, satanic voice, ' 'Yes? Welcome to Hell!'' The others laughed at him. Coming on after all that had been said over the past hour, it made me feel edgy, even though I knew that these were a bunch of eighteen-year-old prats breathing teenage rebellion and defiance.

Somehow, Taylor had managed to squeeze his way to the bar and, over hands waving money and bellowing orders, get a couple of drinks.

'Come on, let's move away from this squeeze,' he said. We carefully threaded our way towards the stage, where there was at least a little bit of standing room. No one was paying any particular attention to the band – rather, they would reach the end of a song and reap a bit of cheering and applause before launching into the next. I watched them rip into a cover of a Tina Turner number, absently tapping my foot as I listened. The number came to an end; cue clapping and whoops.

'Someone's waving at us,' Taylor said. He nodded towards a table in a dark corner. Sitting there were two figures – one was on the large side, and wearing, of all things, some ridiculous confection of a hat, something like an oversized trilby. His companion, who was waving in a limp way, was shorter and slightly less fat, with receding blonde hair and a diamond earring that must have been big, considering how it glittered. The latter pointed at us and waved us over. It was only when we got nearer I realised who it was.

'Hello Dan, long time no see, hun,' he said.

'Hi, Stefan! Well, bugger me!'

'Only if you insist, love.'

Stefan (actually, Stephen, but he insisted on Stefan) Moreton, quite possibly the gayest person in my class at school, years ago.

A man so camp, you could have put scouts on him and called him a Jamboree. He hadn't changed much, apart from a few extra pounds and the hair. He had never been my favourite person, but we'd got along OK, and I hadn't seen him since then. We shook hands, and I introduced him to Taylor. He introduced me to his partner, who so far hadn't said a thing.
'This is Oz. Ignore her – she's being a terrible old queen tonight and not speaking to anyone. Not that you're the most talkative, are you?'
Oz grunted.
'Never mind, he's a sweetie, really. Hasn't long been out of jail – he was a terribly naughty boy, weren't you?'
Another grunt.
'Sooo,' he said, turning back to me and raising an eyebrow, 'what are you doing here? The last I'd heard, you'd run away to foreign climes. I thought you'd have stayed there, away from this dump.'
'Yeah, I was, for quite a while. I'm back for now. Taylor and me travelled together quite a bit.'
I filled in a bit of what I'd been up to, to which Stefan listened politely, but without any real interest, a typical and depressing reaction that I'd gradually grown used to over the past few months.
'What about you?' I asked him eventually.
'Well,' he began, sighing theatrically, 'I've stayed here, in good old Reading. I've got my own place now, a little flat in the ab-so-lutely appropriate Queen Street near the canal. I work for the Prudential, in their IT department.'
'Do you still see any of the others from school?'
'Oh yes, all the time!' And he proceeded to fill me in, in excruciating detail, on who was doing what and where. It seemed that almost all of them had stayed here, married each other, worked in almost identical jobs and lived in identical houses. As I listened, I said a silent prayer of thanks that I hadn't ended up like them.
'You must come and join us at our next meet,' he gushed. 'We're all getting together next week at the Gardener's Arms for Richard's birthday. Look, here's my number,' he continued, scrawling his phone number on a beer mat, 'give me a call and say if you can make it. It'd be great to see you – they'll all be so

interested to see you again.' I took it, but I had no intention of hooking up with them. Most of the people he mentioned had been smug little arseholes while we were at school, and I didn't particularly feel the need to reacquaint myself with their lives – especially if conversation would revolve around children and mortgages.

During all this, Stefan had ignored Taylor completely, but this seemed to suit the latter. He silently smoked his cigarettes, drank his beer, and looked around the bar. At one stage, he was watching the band with what appeared to be a deeply mournful, pensive air; the next he was grinning at nothing in particular, perhaps at just a sudden thought. I drained my own pint.

'Move on?' he said.

'Let's boogie,' I agreed.

We said goodbye to Stefan, me promising to stay in contact, and Oz grunting a farewell, then we got out into the relative coolness of the night.

'Well, I don't know if we're still on Weirdo's course,' said Taylor, 'but that was hot enough to be Hell.'

'You're not joking.'

'Dan, what the Hell is that?' he exclaimed suddenly, pointing at a gleaming metal drum, somewhat taller than either of us, that had risen from the ground next to Queen Victoria while we'd been in the 3 B's.

'That,' I announced, 'is Reading's contribution to town centre, late-night sanitation. It's a pissoir. It rises from the depths late at night in order to stop revellers slashing over the queen.'

'God, so it is', murmured Taylor, going over to inspect its gleaming steel surfaces. Someone had been busy with a knife or a key ring or something; scratched into the surface were phrases like 'poof parlour' and 'gay bar', and, deeply and determinedly gouged, 'I FUCK ARSES'.

'That's actually a good idea. Are there any more?'

'No, that's all.'

'I'll use that on the way back. But for now, where to next?'

'Christ, I don't know – which way do you reckon?'

'Well, how about back this way again?'

He pointed towards Market Place once more.

'Didn't you say there's a good pub up here?'

'The Coopers? Yeah, alright, let's go for that.'
So we staggered round the corner and towards the Coopers. As we were going in, I saw a few women in front of the cash machine outside Barclay's. One of them was smashing it with her shoe, which she had taken off, and was aiming the heel directly at the screen.
'Give – me – my – fucking – card – back – you – fucker!' She screamed, while one of her friends was doubled up laughing.
'Leave it be Leticia,' shouted another, 'I'll lend you some.'
'Fucking machine!' screeched Leticia, before slipping her shoe back on and tottering off with her friends.
'I will say this for Reading,' said Taylor, 'you're never at a loss for entertainment, are you?'

Texts

Where ru?
In da 3Bs innit
How ist?
Gr8 U comin?
L8r U wit NE1
Me & Chas & Bri. Wot bout U?
No 1 @ the mo. U stayin there all night?
No goin to Ice L8r @ 10
Ok M8 cu @ Ice
OK cu l8r bye

Sixteen: Reading is Heaven
Oh beautiful world!

Oscar Wilde

In which the Author, well pleased by the fact that his characters appear to be back on track, goes into another ramble, this time about the joys of reading.

So Dan and Taylor have made it to the Cooper's, meaning that they have completed one circuit of the town this evening. I thought at one stage they weren't going to make it. I have to say, however, that the whole Dantean conceit thing is starting to go a bit awry; In theory, they should be riding the monster Geryon down to the Eighth circle where fraud is punished, and their next stop should involve panders and seducers. How that's going to happen I haven't a clue. Well, I'll just have to cross that bridge when I come to it, I suppose. Of course, by now they are both pretty drunk, so whatever they do now may make no sense whatsoever; However, I think I'll follow them some more tonight and see what happens. I think their pace is beginning to lag somewhat, and who can blame them? They have, after all, been on the go since two o'clock this afternoon, and now it is coming towards ten, with another four hours of boozing ahead of them – plus a late-night kebab and how to get back home. Of course everything's going to be on the woozy side. Dan has already commented on this – the suggestion that Reading is slowly turning into something unrecognisable as the evening progresses. Perhaps it is, perhaps it isn't.

 The observant, interactive reader may have already enquired to him/herself as to the validity of using two voices in this story: Mine as Author, and Dan as narrator. Why on earth two voices? Why not one? Why not many? Why don't we hear an interior monologue from Taylor, for example? Who knows what mysterious, wonderful worlds of thought are going on in his head? Then again, there could be nothing at all. Therein is a problem with any given character, a subject that we touched upon earlier; the eternal presence of The Writer, making His voice known through His mouthpieces. Just as the setting of a tale tells us something about the interests and preoccupations of the Author, so what the characters say and how they say it, or rather how skilfully they are made to say it, reflects the writer's psyche, concerns, hopes and fears. Too often, the silent character is an empty one, a pawn waiting to be activated at the appropriate point of the tale. What story arc do characters follow when the spotlight is not on them? This is, of course, a question Stoppard asks in Rosencrantz and Guildenstern are dead. But have you ever applied the same question as you have read a novel? When the plot follows one set of characters, what are the others doing? Are they left to, as it were, lay in the dark, in the same place as they were left, until they are needed once more? Do they live outside the plot? Likewise, have you ever considered this of the people you see and meet every day? Do they have an existence outside the narrative arc of your own story? Your nearest and dearest do, yes; perhaps also the man in the corner shop, or your work colleagues. But what about the woman who sat opposite you on the bus into work this morning? How about the young local couple you once saw when you were on holiday that time, the two of them strolling arm in arm along the beach? What about the lonely, sad-looking old lady you spied sitting on the train platform? Were they, are they, real? Day after day, we encounter thousands of people, some more, some less; they enter our personal stories for perhaps a brief moment, like glimmers of light on dark water, and are gone, as if they never existed. Yet exist they do, and each has innumerable stories within them, countless tales that you are unlikely ever to hear. The interactive reader, however, can infer tales and myths from everyone and everything he or she meets; For the world itself, our mundane, plodding world, is glittering with unread stories, just waiting for the right person to come along and understand. And hence the title I've given this interlude – Reading is Heaven.

Now, just as in a previous chapter I said that the real, brick-and-mortar Reading that our heroes find themselves in is not Hell, so equally it is not Paradise – I don't think anyone in their right mind would ever claim that. Besides, descriptions of heaven are notorious sketchy; consider that the Divine Comedy loses steam the minute the Pilgrim and the Poet climb Satan's shaggy flanks and leave Hell. This is because we are immeasurably better at imagining the worst possible things that can befall us than thinking of the best. No, despite claims to the contrary, Heaven is not a place on Earth. But reading can be heaven, or as near as it is possible for us to imagine. When we pick up a book, the minute we open it to the first page, we enter another universe, another cosmos, created for our pleasure and delectation. It may be limited in scope, breadth or vision, but it is still complete by its own terms. And if the whole of anything is good, how can it be anything else but Heaven? And just as the physical world we move in is both replete with and devoid of meanings coiled within meanings, so can a book, and as such is a potential source of endless pleasure; and that, I think, is just about as close a definition of paradise as is available to us. You see, unlike Dan, or even Taylor, you don't even need to travel beyond the confines of your armchair in order to see what there is beyond – a good book and a readiness to read in an attentive way are enough.

Seventeen: saints and slappers
There is no such thing as society.
                                             Margaret Thatcher.

Oh Fuck off.
                         Most right-thinking people in reply.
In which our two chums take a well-deserved opportunity to relax in a quiet corner; they chew the fat in a way only the terminally drunk can; things seem to get stranger.

After the heaving scrum of the three B's, the Cooper's was a quiet haven in comparison. It was still quite full, but not so bad that we couldn't get a seat. It was a relief, to be honest; I was feeling the strain of the day, and just for a few minutes at least, I just wanted to be somewhere relatively calm and relaxed. We got a couple of beers and took up seats near the wide open windows so we could enjoy the balmy night air, filled with the scents of petrol fumes, cheap colognes, vomit, and people shouting at each other.
'I used to come here a lot before I went abroad,' I said, apropos of nothing. ' It was pretty good then – bikers, punks, Goths, and lots of noisy music on the juke box, as long as you could handle 'Bat Out of Hell' and The Doors being played at least twice each evening. Then they tried to change it into a winebar, with a smart clientele and bouncers on the door. Thankfully, that fucked up, and now it's starting to get back to what it was.'
'Looks pretty old.'
'yeah, I think it's one of the oldest buildings still standing in the centre – then again, I think all this timber is probably all mock Tudorbethan crap.'
Taylor pulled out his pack of fags, and dropped the last two on the table. We lit up, and gazed blankly out into the night.
'This view's not a patch on Beirut.'
'No.'
Three men sprinted past the window, going hell for leather, closely followed by a police car with its siren blaring. In the background, someone, possibly some remnant from the old Cooper's days, had put on The Door's 'The End'. I looked around the bar; a couple of sad-looking fat blokes were propped at the

bar itself, smoking roll-ups; a girl was crying in a corner, being comforted by her friend; the barmaid was discussing something earnestly with a couple of people in a language I didn't recognise; four office workers were roaring their heads off and slopping their drinks over the table; and Taylor was still looking, somewhat sadly I thought, into the night.

'Dan, have we changed?' He asked suddenly.

I shrugged. 'I don't know. Don't think so, not really.'

'yet we do, don't we?' he continued. 'Look, this afternoon, I saw you and thought how miserable you looked, how weary of this world. Now we're here, and I already notice awkward silences. Why?'

'It's 'cos we're pissed, mostly,' I replied. 'We've drunk far too much. Besides we haven't seen each other in four years, and that's a long time of travelling in different directions, you know. I've been my place, you've been yours. And we shall tell each other what we have done and what we have seen, the minute we can speak and think coherently. But we haven't changed, not really.'

'Places change people,' Taylor said, slowly. 'They, well, they impinge upon them. If you stay in one place all your life, you stay as one kind of person, thinking in one kind of way, having one set of opinions. But when you travel, then something alters, something in the soul.'

I considered this.

'Not necessarily,' I started. 'I reckon it depends on the person. If you want your eyes opened, then they will. Perhaps you don't need to travel for that, but then again that movement is the key to it. You know, what you said earlier – change perspective and all that.'

"Thou hast said it", he grinned, then flashed a smiling look at me. Suddenly, he was reanimated. 'It's perspective that's the thing, then. You're down because of what, exactly? Just being here?'

'Well, yes. No. I don't know.'

'I'd say that it's all down to what you see this place as – from what you said earlier, I reckon this is your jail. Am I right?'

I didn't say anything, but I didn't need to.

'Well, let me give you my view. I travelled by train early on this morning, travelling through landscape that lay under a sultry haze, through a landscape that gleamed silver because of being chalk land. The train arrived in the outskirts of this town, and I had to wonder, because it seemed like a Midlands industrial city and I had come too far north. But no, I then saw these fine buildings over and around the river, and towards what I now understand to be the centre, and a phrase from Daniel Defoe's tour of England came to mind. True, it wasn't that promising, especially being greeted by that grey lump of a building opposite the station, but definitely no worse than many other places I've been. Having found a bus that would take me to Emmer Green, I had a pleasant lunchtime ride up, crossing a river full of life and heading towards a place that, at first sight, seemed to be a forest with a few houses interspersed. Oh yeah, it's not like that for real, but at a distance that's how it seemed. The same happened after I'd met you and we were coming back down; I looked into the bowl that holds this place, and saw a city mainly composed of trees.'

'Try seeing it in winter, then,' I muttered

'But I didn't, and probably never will, and just saw this place on a bright warm day, when it is possessed, even superficially, of beauty. And now, staggering round here as we are, I see that this town is stark, staring mad – it's full of drunk eccentrics and people who not only wish they were somewhere else, but also that they were someone else. That's why they indulge in houses that are too extravagant and cars they can't afford. I quite like it. And now, to add to the mad fun, we have your fucking weirdo, insisting that we are in Hell, and that all this is some kind of metaphysical concoction for our pleasure. So far, you must agree, we've been massively entertained, and apart from the ale, we haven't paid for any of it….talking of which….'

He lumbered to his feet before I could even begin to frame a reply, and headed for the fruit machine, which someone was just walking away from with a look of resigned disgust on their face. I realised that Taylor must have had his eye surreptitiously on the guy for a while, and was waiting to pounce. He was talking arrant balls, of course, I thought, then rapidly unthought it. This was still old Taylor, my friend, and his discursive, argumentative, inquisitive ways. Alright, he could be seen as a bullshitter, but that was only in a certain light – the same that cast a dreary, judgemental light on where I lived. Was he right? Was where I was having an effect on what I saw and perceived? Just then, I got an image of Beattie in my head, and my heart and guts lunged with desire for her. I realised how much I missed her; seeing Taylor, and knowing that he'd actually talked with her only a matter of fourteen days ago, triggered everything off : You know, all that maudlin clichéd crap, of first meeting, going out, the last time I saw her, and so on. The fact is, we never quite got it together, for one reason or another; We always wanted to, but work commitments and circumstance always prevented us. The truth is, I'd begun to doubt her feelings for me, even after the last time we'd met, but Taylor's appearance and comment had renewed hopes and feelings I hadn't felt for months. She was still thinking of me, still had feelings for me. I clung to that idea like some lovesick teenager – but that's the way I felt! It was, on the face of it, somewhat ridiculous, and I told myself so: we were on opposite sides of the planet, after all. But so what? I had begun to give up hope of ever meeting someone again after my first marriage, done and finished while disastrously young, and the catalyst for my travels abroad. Then I had met her while at a particularly low point, and it was as if the sunlight had pierced a fierce gloom of cloud. I lost myself in a reverie of her now. I found a last cigarette in my own pack, lit up, and looked out into the street. People were walking along in various stages of inebriation, shouting out instructions to go to this place or that, or laughing, or doing nothing much more than a slow amble. And in the midst of them all, standing under the market obelisk, was The Fucking Weirdo. He was grinning at me, and giving me the thumbs up. I gave him the finger, but he carried on grinning, and pointed to his left, towards the town centre. He mouthed the words 'keep going', then moved off himself. I put my head out the window, but he'd already disappeared into the gloom. Now that was another thing; his insistence that we were in some kind of story. Well, from a philosophical viewpoint, I could kind of understand that. From the point of view that he was in some way manipulating my actions and I had bugger all to do except follow on passively, speak only when required, move only when desired, that was unacceptable. Who the fuck did he think he was? It was glaringly obvious he was following us around and

backfilling a story for us wasn't it? Then again, in my drunken state, I started pondering how many people had watched us today, how many sets of eyes and street-corner cameras had been trained on our movements. Indeed, I'd noticed the unobtrusive CCTV cameras in this pub, and grew, I admit, somewhat paranoid about who might be watching me even now. My nervous train of thought was broken by a triumphant 'Yes!' from Taylor, and the merry chinking of money from the fruit machine. He scooped up his winnings and came back over.
'Look at that,' he said, 'I reckon that's our evening nearly paid for, along with what I got earlier. See – chance favours the well-prepared mind.'
'Good for you. The Weirdo's back – I saw him outside while you were unburdening that thing.'
'Fuck him, who cares? More beer?'
'Let's make it a short, and get out of here. And fags.'
'Of course.'
He went to get some cigarettes, just as a group of lads more or less fell through the door, shouting and laughing. They picked themselves up, and rushed for the bar, yelling for beer.
'All right, all right, don't panic!' the bar manageress said curtly. 'You'll all get served – who's rattled your cages then, eh?' She poured them beer, while they continued their rather witless conversation at full volume.
'Yeah, well I'll 'ave your sister,' bellowed one.
'You're welcome to 'er,' replied another.
'But she don't cook a breakfast as well as 'is mother!' joined in a third, all of them laughing hard. I couldn't be arsed to listen to them, although it was wearyingly noisy, and basically involved who they were going to shag and when, or triumphant conquests. Just another bunch of shouty boys, I thought, hiding their fear under their swagger. An image of one of them coming on to Beattie went through my mind like dirty water, and made me momentarily angry, before I put it away again.
'Noisy fuckwits, aren't they?' said Taylor, sitting back down with a couple of vodkas.
'Could not have put it better myself, Taylor, could not have put it better myself.' I paused, then asked him.
'Taylor, be honest, really – how was Beattie?'

'Dan, I told you. She's good. She's happy. She is not seeing anyone, if I understand that to be the answer to the question you really wanted to ask. And, if you ask me, I would say that she misses you. But if you really want to find out, I suggest you communicate with her. Send her an email. Ask her how she feels, not me. I can only guess; she's the one to tell you what you want to know. What's the matter? Afraid she's going to say no, reject you? Maybe she will, but mooching round here won't help you find out anything.'

'Yeah, you're right, as ever.'

'OK, you lost each other, but you can still get it on. It's up to the pair of you. You are not glued to Reading, she is not stuck to Bangkok. You can choose. Just don't expect me to play sodding Cupid.'

He grinned.

'I reckon this place has sucked the risk-taker out of you. That's the one problem with England – unless you're careful, it blanches all the spirit from you, like some kind of psychic vampire, and you end up as bland as all the rest.'

I grunted, then knocked back my vodka. I suddenly felt really annoyed with him.

'Right then,' I said, 'let's get going. Knock it back and let's do it. Shall we take a risk, then? What do you reckon?'

'Chill out! I didn't say you'd become boring, Dan. I didn't mean that at all.'

'Yeah, it didn't sound like it,' I said nastily.

'Oh come on, man, you know that's not true..'

The whole thing threatened to descend into the kind of drunken row that makes people not talk to each other for ever after, but fortunately we were saved by none other than The Weirdo, who suddenly appeared by the window.

'Hello,' he said.

'Fuck off, you twat,' I replied.

'There's no need for that,' he said, looking somewhat crestfallen.

'Look, what is your problem?' said Taylor. 'Why are you following us around? Amusing though your little idea is, it is becoming tiresome. Now, as my good friend said, fuck off, you twat, and preferably go and die.' He stood up, and made to grab the Weirdo, who pulled back, and said,

'Keep moving – look out for the next malbolge!'
He disappeared again, leaving both of us looking at each other.
'The next what?' we both said, then laughed.
'Do you reckon he makes a habit of stalking people?'
'Could well be,' I said. 'He obviously doesn't have any friends. Come on, let's get out of here.'
I went to have a slash. The bogs were in an absolutely foul condition – some complete arse had managed to flood the thing, so there was a lake of piss and god knows what else. Going into the gents, I passed a chap, who, in the middle of this reek, was trying to pull! He was chatting to a pissed-looking girl, saying
'Yeah, you know, you're looking really fit – I like your dress, it makes you look dead hot an' all...'
The girl was half-listening, and half-occupied with pulling something from her hair. Only on returning did I realise it was chunks of vomit.
'What's the time?' I asked Taylor as he finished off his drink.
'Not quite half-ten,' he said. 'Where to next?'
We walked out the door and back onto the street. I was feeling deeply unsteady.
'Somewhere with music, maybe? I know; let's go to one of those bars in the Oracle, then we must and shall go to either the Turtle or The After Dark, or maybe both. Come on, this way.'
And we wandered down Market Place, past the bank and Oxfam, towards Duke Street again.

MO'S KEBABS

OPEN 1.00 – LATE

LAMB AND CHICKEN DONER KEBAB

BURGERS

CHIPS

SALADS

SOFT DRINKS

DONER KEBAB

SMALL - £2.50

MEDIUM - £3.00

LARGE - £ 3.50

CHICKEN DONER - £3.00

HAMBURGER - £2.80

CHEESEBURGER - £3.10

DOUBLE BURGER £5.00

CHIPS - £1.00

LARGE PORTION - £1.50

SALAD - £1.50

CANNED DRINKS - £1.00

Eighteen: weariness
'Tis a tale told by an idiot, signifying nothing.

Shakespeare

More desperate mugging from the Author.
Well, there had to be at least one Shakespeare quote somewhere in these introductions. I must say, I think Dan and Taylor were really rather rude to me in the previous chapter, particularly the latter – I expected much better of him. Of course, it's not me per se, just a characterisation of me, just as the me writing this isn't really me, if you catch my drift. Just as meanings nestle within each other, so levels of character hide within others, like Russian Babushka dolls. I'm no longer sure myself of what's going on; I thought I had the hang of it, a while back, but now I realise that I was being mislead, quite possibly by myself. The truth is, I am tired, I am weary; I want to leave my story, but how can I when I'm only halfway through?

Imagine those times when you have been exhausted; think back to when you have been so worn out that you just want to drop off there and then, but because of circumstances you can't. Perhaps you are in your car, driving mile after mile on a motorway, your home still distant; It might be that it's the end of a big night out, and you've missed your last bus and you can't get a taxi for love or money, while the heavens open, and you have to walk slowly home in the wet; maybe it's mid-afternoon on a Thursday in the working week, and you are longing for the weekend to come and release you from your misery, while the second hand crawls round the clock. At these times, when all you really want to do is curl into a ball and shut the world out, how do you keep going? What motivates you to drive those weary miles, plod those tiresome steps, file that dreary work? And it is likewise for the Author. You can see, ever so distantly, the point at which the narrative will end; perhaps it is still many thousands of words away, but it is there, as tangible as the notion of home; I want to drive on to the end, yet know that there are many twists and curves left, and you, the reader, are welcome to join me. As I mentioned much earlier on, you are lucky inasmuch as you can leisurely skip these detours of mine, and even plough straight onto the last page by the expediency of flicking through the entire book. Lucky you: I do not have that luxury, having been fool enough to turn myself into a character in my own creation, and therefore have to wait for the narrative to take its ponderous course. And at the same time, I must guide it as well, being the writer. So how will I continue?

I could, of course, end it all at a stroke, by merely writing something like, 'I changed my mind, and told Taylor to flag down a taxi; we got in it and went back to my house, where we slept.' The End. However, that would be a colossal cheat, and leave both you and I dissatisfied with the entire thing. Likewise, I could employ the old 'and suddenly I woke up and realised that it was all a dream' con trick, which would leave a sour taste in the mouth as well. Perhaps I could murder everyone, but that would be defying the narrative's internal logic. No, plod on I must, and keep thinking, even though I am far from my goal still, that there will be an end, and I will reach it. And as for you, dear reader, when you are next stuck in a situation you want to get out of, when next it is Thursday afternoon in the office or the rain is pelting your bare head, imagine these things; Tom Jones, just after he has been thrown out of his home by his adoptive father, Allworthy, wondering where he is to go; The runner Pheidippides, sprinting from Marathon to bring the news of the Persians' defeat to the people of Athens, his mouth gaping dry and his feet sore, his heart thumping wildly and the thought in his mind of whether he will ever see home; My great-great uncle, a soldier in the first world war, lying in the mud of the Somme after the first great push, his arm shattered by a German bullet and his entire company lying dead around him, wondering if he will ever be rescued and get home again; An illegal immigrant smuggled into the country, working on some colossal field in East Anglia, who lifts his aching back straight and shivers in his cheap clothes, looking eastwards to where his family are, hundreds or thousands of miles away. Look at their faces in your mind's eye; Do you see the similarity? Do you see how the weariness in the face, the frown and the look in their eyes makes them resemble each other? Now look up in a mirror quickly, and you will catch the same image, the fraternal expression. Yes, you may be caught and tired, but you know you will reach home, and your problems are nowhere near as big as theirs; the figures I've just invoked don't know whether they will or not. And I, likewise, feel the same right now. I plod along, wondering what's coming next; in the story, I follow our two heroes, ensuring they fulfil the imaginary plot sequence I have cast for them. And so we zoom back on them to find out what's going on.

Nineteen: Deeper through the night
Twas brillig, and the slithy tothes outgrabe the mimsy borogoves.

Edmund Lear.

Dan and Taylor head towards the Oracle once more; what they see on the way; they are not impressed by the bar they go into; what they see as they leave; they have an encounter with the porphyry chelonian.

Crossing Duke Street Bridge again, I noticed that the beggars from before had gone. Instead, there was just one guy on the bridge itself, playing a flute, with a dog laid curled up next to him. He was playing a lively Irish tune, and a few people were giving him money. I dug out a quid and gave it to him.
'He'll probably spend it on drugs,' I said to Taylor.
'He can spend it on what he likes, it's his money now.'
Outside the brightly lit Oracle, there was a merry chaos of people. One group of lads were pushing a couple of their friends in wheely bins. They'd been stuck in headfirst, and their legs were waving wildly, much to the amusement of passers-by. On the footbridge, a troop of girls were attempting to walk backwards in single file, and by and large failing dismally, falling over each other and dissolving in raucous shrieking laughter. Everywhere there was a hustle and roar as diners left the restaurants and headed for the various nightclubs on the south bank of the river that bifurcated the centre. Music thumped and rose from them; queues were forming to get into some. We walked past the hum and chat and the odd scuffle until we got to Bar Med
'Let's give this a go,' I said. We waited in line for a couple of minutes then entered. Inside, it was even hotter than the three B's had been and very dark. Silhouettes thronged the bar, which stretched across the far wall, and the dance floor, sandwiched between alcoves near us and a raised seating area. Figures writhed to the music, while others watched them from the platform, the lights flickering upward into their faces and casting demonic shadows. We struggled to the bar, and were eventually given exorbitantly-priced lager. There was nowhere

to sit, so we joined the other sad souls round the dance floor and watched the general writhing and excuses for dancing. One bloke's moves seemed to consist solely of jumping up and down, waving one hand in the air. There was a man of about the same age as me who was doing what can only be called 'Dad Dancing', namely staying in one spot and vaguely waving the limbs around in approximate time with the music. I pointed him out to Taylor.

'There's the reason I stopped dancing after I was thirty-one. It becomes genetically impossible to dance properly once you're past your twenties.'

'And there is something that I thought only happened in legends.'

Taylor was pointing at a circle of six women. They were actually dancing round their handbags.

I looked round at the other observers. I noticed that they were almost all men, and most had a leering, hungry look to them. They clutched their drinks, and nodded along to the beat of the music.

'Look at this lot,' said Taylor, 'watching the floor show, and too afraid to be shown up to join in. It's always amused me how men in this country are scared stiff of moving in what might be an unsightly way – they're so damn afraid of their bodies. I'll tell you what'll happen to them – they'll drink their own body weight in lager and then try to latch onto some girl at the end of the evening, slurring something about a nice slow dance. Then, once they've got some hapless girl on the floor, they'll throw up all down the back of their dresses.'

'Don't think you're far wrong there.'

Watching all this inept dancing reminded me of its antithesis: the grace of belly dancers I'd seen in various places from Cairo to Istanbul, and the good-natured, wholly amateur but deeply graceful circle dance I'd seen a whole wedding party spontaneously do one warm evening in Antakya.

'Why is it we're so crap at dancing, do you reckon?'

'What I said. Fear. Fear of the body, fear of standing out, fear of being different in the wrong way – oh yeah, you can have as many piercings and tattoos as you like, as long as your mates have the same, but you're not really being different. Have a good look at everyone – notice that they are all, to some extent

or other, afraid. That's why they drink, and shout, and laugh as loud as they can. It's why English people blot themselves out every weekend. They're afraid of having to face themselves in the mirror, or that eternal bogeyman, the neighbour, as in 'what will the neighbours think?' We spend too much time worrying about the good opinion of others when the fact of the matter is that it's generally not worth a stuff. And if it's an opinion based merely on what you look like, or what you do, then it really isn't worth a stuff. If you look carefully, you'll see that mark of anxiety in every face when its owner thinks no one is looking.'
I watched, and yes, it seemed that what Taylor said was true; here and there, between swigs of lager and puffs on fags, between snatched bites of conversation or laughter, when no one was watching, then on faces would appear glimmers of anxiety, of worry – no more than momentary, but there nonetheless. I watched for these changes intently, and wondered what it was these people had to be worried about. It seemed suddenly as if I was looking at a fresh page of text, one that talked of a secret unnamed fear that stalked everyone, and I realised it must have been written large all over my face when Taylor had walked into the White Horse earlier on. Wondering about the worry in others' faces made me face up to what it may be that had unsettled me so much over the last few months. It was fear of being trapped, of being robbed of choice, of being assimilated into the great stream of the everyday and the commonplace. The same fear that had driven me abroad in the first place, if truth be told. But now, seeing it everywhere, flitting from face to face like the shadow of a wind-driven cloud over land, I wondered at myself, for being so in thrall to so little a thing. And the persistent gloom of the last few months, even through my drunkenness, began to lift. Even the mild paranoia of being followed by the Weirdo started dissipating.

'Everyone's afraid,' I said suddenly.

'That's about the long and the short of it,' Said Taylor. 'We're all scared of something. The thing is, though, the simple fact of knowing that makes the fear recede.'

'So what about you?'

Taylor paused, then grinned.

'I worked it out ages ago, so I'm not really frightened anymore, not even of going grey, losing my looks and eventually dying.

I've accepted that; lots of guys can't. No, the only thing that makes me afraid now is of being trapped, and I'm damned if I'm going to let that happen.' He spread his arms out wide, nearly poking someone in the eye with his beer bottle, and said, smiling broadly, 'and for tonight, there is nothing and no one who can bring us down, Dan! No fucking way!'

'Too fucking right!' We clinked bottles, then slugged them back. The heat was overbearing, and the DJ had cranked the sound up, so the music was getting the same way. I could feel the bassbeat thudding all through me. Taylor shouted something to me, but I couldn't make out a word of what he said. He repeated it, I still couldn't understand, so I motioned him towards the bar.

'..I said, let's get the fuck out of here, it's too noisy,' he said.

'It'll all be like this now, wherever we go.'

'Whatever – this isn't exactly my cup of tea anyway. Where are the bogs here?'

We went together, up a set of stairs and almost over a comatose young man who was lying spreadeagled on them in a splatter of spew.

'I can see that Reading is not only an unending source of entertainment, its citizens know how to have a damn good time,' Taylor muttered to me as we stepped gingerly over the body and between the chunks on the way back down. We weaved our way through the now completely packed club and into the relative cool of the night. The moon had risen, and there was just a hint of a breeze, but one carrying warning of a storm to come. Just outside, there was a girl sobbing her eyes out to her friend.

'What am I going to do now?' she wailed. 'It had all my money in and my mobile. And my credit card. How am I going to get home?'

Her friend was soothing her, saying 'Don't worry, we'll get back somehow. We'll have to find a policeman first. I can't believe how it got nicked. I really thought our stuff'd be safe if we danced round it..'

We walked past the Jelly Legg'd Chicken arts centre and up to the main road, turning right and heading up towards St. Mary's. As we passed over the Kennet once more, I pointed westwards and said,

'we could follow this all the way to Bristol, you know.'
'How far?'
'About eighty miles.'
'It's a bit late for that. Everything'll be closed by the time we get there.'
'True. Let's go this way then.'
'Where to?'
'Where else? The Turtle!'
We walked up the road, past the bland offices and to the corner of St Mary's, Minster Street, and Castle Street. We turned right, and walked, or more accurately staggered, past the Fez Club, to the whooping queue of young and old waiting to enter the legendary Purple Turtle bar. Three bouncers greeted punters cheerily, and courteously looked in any bags they were carrying.
'Welcome to the Turtle,' I said.
'This looks more the thing,' replied Taylor. 'Good, is it?'
'That's one way of putting it,' I said. 'I still think this is one of the best. I used to come here when it was somewhere else.'
Taylor looked at me, perplexed, so I explained.
'This is the New Turtle. The Old Turtle was in a condemned building on the site of what is now the Oracle – in particular, Brannigan's nightclub. It was tiny – it probably held about 150 safely, but it generally had about 500 in. There were two bogs that were so befouled and vile that they developed a sentient life of their own. You virtually had to catch the damn things before pissing in them. And the atmosphere, Taylor, ah shit, you just couldn't capture it now – it was something special. People dancing on the bar tops, squirting drinks into waiting mouths. The best juke box that I have ever seen. Beer from round the world. Occasionally, Danny, that's the boss, he would book a band, who would perform on the world's tiniest stage and try not to fall off or destroy their own equipment. Posters plastered over every surface. It was something special, then; It's still not bad – worth the crack, anyway.'
'Now that's the first time I've heard you get really enthusiastic about anything all night, Dan,' said Taylor, smiling, 'but now it comes back to me that you've actually mentioned this place before. I think it was in Goa: We were on the beach, waiting for the dawn, and you were raving about it in pretty much the same way then – I remember you made me feel what it was like, it's

texture and shape on a wet night. And now here we are in the flesh. Well, it's certainly purple.'

We came to the head of the queue, the bouncers greeted us, and we entered the turtle's lair.

Twenty: Are you yourself?

They were sitting around, arguing whether the cow was really there.

E.M. Forster

In which The Author seeks to prove that he really exists, in terms of the story and in terms of real life.

Earlier on, I mentioned about how we present different facets of ourselves to our different acquaintances, that the many-leaved book of the self is open on different pages as we see fit. What are the consequences of abruptly showing your nearest and dearest a whole new chapter? The obvious one is complete bafflement. We've all read those news items about the unassuming family man, and incidentally it is almost always men, who suddenly go crazy and run off with someone thirty years their junior, or who start calling themselves Justine and change sex, or butcher everyone within a two hundred metre radius. Their story is plastered over the news for a day or two, and always there is the same refrain, from some neighbour or relative, saying *it was so out of character. It was as if he became someone else.* But the fact of the matter is that it was in character, the poor unfortunate was himself – it's just that he never realised it, or no one else did. Taylor asked earlier on whether he and Dan had changed. And despite assertions to the contrary, despite our boasts of still feeling eighteen or whatever, we do change; Our characters evolve as surely as the earth beneath our feet is moulded by the climate, by upheaval and eruption, by our very feet walking over it, and there is damn all one can do to reverse that fact. If we want to revert to what we once were, all we can do is make a poor imitation of it. The past, the more it recedes, becomes almost as unknowable as the future, albeit more accessible via the faulty vision that is memory. Think of those fancy-dress parties where you dress up as you looked when you were a teenager; Do you actually resemble that past self, down to the last detail, or is it a mere ghost of what was? Taylor and Dan have changed, even if they have not noticed it – as Dan said, they have wandered down their various paths, and had their characters moulded by what they have done and seen. Taylor never used to be the cool, analytical person he is now. The part of him that is calm and observant has contributed considerably of course, but the rest is a combination of circumstance, opportunity and education. It is an interesting thing, but our personalities are in part determined by happenstance and serendipity. This gradual change in persona doesn't get remarked upon, except when we suddenly encounter someone, an old schoolmate or lover for instance, after years of being apart, and during an evening of catching up, they suddenly say *how you've changed!* Or the wife in a relationship that has crumbled gradually without either person being aware, who reviews the foundations of what is left, looks back in the looking glass of the mind, and reproves her soon-to-be ex-husband with the words *You've changed. You're not the man you were,* without commenting on how she too has altered. The person who goes thug, however, seems to have been the same since forever, but then comes the apocalyptic day when his character erupts, and something fearsome, unknown, even bestial, emerges.

Why are people so afraid of change? It happens, and surely we don't want to remain children all our lives. In order to live, we must needs change, because that which does not change, does not live.

Likewise, stories evolve too. The ideas I set out at the beginning have altered as I have written, and the characters of Dan and Taylor, as I have penned them, have hardened from mere wisps into something far more tangible. What I had planned has not happened, and I find that the people and the story itself have somehow taken over. Now, this is not on: surely I should be in control of it all? Ah, but I also explained that I am unreliable as a narrator, prone to error and no sure guide. In this, I am quite unlike the metaphysical guide that is Taylor, or his original, Virgil in Inferno, who of course is Dante the writer, not Dante the Pilgrim or Dante the character in The Comedy, giving himself another disguise. I am Author, but not the controlling voice or hand of the real writer. As such, I am getting confused, and I'm sure I'm not the only one; Do I really exist; And if I do, have I also changed during the course of this book? Of course, in the narrative itself, I have made no more than fleeting appearances, but I suspect I'll be saying a lot more before long. Yet how can I know that, if I can't foresee what'll happen next, being a character in the story? As character, I don't seem to have altered much, primarily because I have been viewed through the lens of Dan's narrative skills, and of course this is only over the course of one night. One important alteration, however, has been the placing of a name: I started off as 'fucking weirdo', then I became 'The Fucking Weirdo', and now plain old 'The Weirdo'. Of course, I have been pigeonholed by Dan's perspective of me, to which I really should object, but at least I have a name, unlike many of the bit players littering this story; Imagine a cast list at the end, listing them all! What would that look like?

What is more irksome, from the point of being pigeonholed, is the fact that I have done it to myself, if you see what I mean. Here I am, writing the story, using these interludes as a kind of framework within which is the story, in which I use another's voice who views me from their perspective, and then only rare glimpses. Where does 'I' begin and end? My problem is this, now; Do I, the Author, actually exist? Obviously, Dan and Taylor et al are artificial constructs, even if they are becoming progressively more real, and the setting, while based solidly on fact, is still an artificial environment. From their perspective, however, I cannot exist: If I am the Great Hand, ordering round their every move, deeming as and when they should speak, they necessarily are unreal, which from the perspective of the great 'I' is untenable and unpalateable. If, on the other hand, they are becoming more real as the story progresses, it therefore follows that I must, as a narrative voice, begin to decline and disappear, be reduced to a whispering shadow, unless I take a more central role in the story itself. However, by doing that, while I may become more 'real' in terms of the story, I would have a limited existence, being constrained by the terms and conditions of the narrative's internal logic and physics. Not only that, I would be rendered through Dan's looking-glass, and so you would only see a distorted me. Likewise, I would render myself fictional in the terms of the reader's universe. I would, as it were, be like some exhibited thing in a zoo, prowling a fake jungle behind glass.

So the question is, what to do? Shall I remain the clown in the interlude, performing for the benefits of the audience, or shall I enter the tale proper, and stop making quick on-and-off appearances? I lose out either way. The point I'm making, I suppose, is that any narrative that involves a first-person account must needs be dominated by the ego, which sees what it wishes to see and no more, whilst a more distanced approach is clearly a fabrication, based on the Author's Deity-like status to be omniscient and omnipotent in terms of the tale's universe. As I have mentioned repeatedly however, I am at the whim of the story, and I can't be sure what it's going to throw at me next.

But returning to the story, I feel we are drawing ever closer to whatever it is that Taylor and Dan are trying to reach, whether it be paradise or some state of drunken Nirvana, or just as low as it's possible to reach. Friday night is reaching its climax, and Saturday is not far off. For now, they are in the legendary Purple Turtle and its wild frenzy of life; In terms of the Dantean plot, they are still in the Eighth Circle, roundabout the counsellors of fraud. I must admit, though, that the plotting has begun to go awry, as far as I can perceive, and right now there is only the merest suggestion of The Comedy peering through – further evidence, if any were needed, that my story is gaining its own weight as it progresses. Whether the old plot shall be jettisoned entirely is still open to speculation.

Twenty-one: Flame, sword and plague
And, like a speaking tongue vibrant to frame
Language, the tip of it flickering to and fro
Threw out a voice and answered:

Dante Alighieri

Our drunken duo savour the delights of the Purple Turtle; They witness the merry and motley crowd therein; They see examples of fraud, violence and forgery, all in the name of having fun.

The place was utterly heaving, there's no other word for it. People jostled their way through here, there and everywhere, some heading for the bogs, others to the downstairs bar, most to the main bar or on into the garden.
'Whoah, it's like going into your past, this place,' said Taylor. ' Student city.' He admired the turtle-and-UFO inspired mural and the hundreds of posters plastered to the walls, many of which hadn't been changed since the place opened.
' Yeah, it's kind of extremely distilled youth. That's why you get anybody and everybody passing through, some giving, some drinking.'
As if to prove the point, two late middle-aged guys waddled past, wheezing their way to the bar; they had sad, saggy faces and straggly grey moustaches, hairstyles that had seen better days, and beer guts that acted like cowcatchers as they ambled through the crowd. At the same time, a crew of five or six lithe young women, no older than nineteen, and wearing fairy wings and halos, jiggled past to the spiral staircase leading downwards. Two women the wrong side of fifty, their hairstyles coiffed and dyed with pink fringes and wearing dresses that must have taken a lot of bravery to put on, wafted by, laughing with smoke-cracked voices about how they were going to pull tonight; A few remnants of the office crowd, their suits and ties stained and wrought, staggered through the joyous melee, clutching half-drunk lagers to their chests; a massive biker bloke, beard forked in Viking style, waded through, determined to get something to drink; a goth couple, him in long black trenchcoat, shades and black hat, her in bright red hair and leather corset, lace gloves and thigh-length boots, drifted coolly

by; one of Reading's oldest punks, a man who had once sported a stunning blond mohican two feet tall, but was now reduced to two spiky tufts above each ear, swaggered through in his faded punk finery; and milling around was the great press of people, still thirsty, still hungering after the fierce joy of a damn good Friday night out on the town, and we were among them, that late night spark of desire was lit, we were flying, and would stay so until we were kicked out of the last bar just after two in the morning. But for now, we were caught up in the rush of the time, and being sucked slowly towards the bar by the sheer press of people.

'I must say, this place is buzzy,' Taylor commented. 'It, shall I say, fucking rocks. It has an edge. I like here. Is it always thus?'

'Must have picked a good night. Sometimes, it feels like some kind of theme park for the middle-aged to come and revisit their lost youth. That's now, anyway: It was seriously cool a decade ago. Even so, it still has its moments.' We edged closer to the bar. 'The problem with getting booze is, however, perennial. The queue is always about five deep. Get ready to squeeze in where you can, wave cash and grin nicely.'

The Clash were playing at full volume on the juke box, the atmosphere reeked of sweat, alcohol, fags and cannabis, and it was misty too. I managed to get my arm onto a tiny section of the bar that was sticky with god knows what – it was never wise to enquire anyway, and thankfully the lights were set to low. A boy and a girl next to me saw each other, smiled into each other's eyes, then fell to kissing ferociously against a handy pillar. One of the bar staff on pot duty lifted the service flap, carefully repositioned the couple with a smile so they weren't obstructing it, then went off to gather glasses. Another bar man yelled at me for my order.

'Two pints of Kronenbourg.' I had to yell to try and make myself understood, and in the end I gestured at the pump to get what I wanted. Two pints and several pounds lighter I managed to escape, only to find Taylor, who'd been drifted up to the far end of the bar by the tide of humanity pushing onwards, standing with two pints himself.

'Well, it'll save time. Let's find a safe corner somewhere.'

We managed to lodge ourselves in a corner with the bass bin of the sound system, next to the fruit machine, a perfect vantage point to watch the ebbing and flowing of the drinkers.
'What's through there?' Taylor enquired, pointing to the door in the rear wall of the building.
'That's through to the garden. There's another bar there, and heaters and stuff. It's more of a yard than a garden – I very much doubt that any plants'd survive long there. In winter, they put up a big pavilion so they can carry on using it. That way,' I continued, pointing towards the spiral staircase near the front, takes you to the downstairs bar – it's supposed to be dance-oriented, but it ends up as packed as here. Round the corner's the bogs.'
The music changed: now it was Blur, 'Parklife'. A group in front of us started to sing along, picking out one of their own, who was on the lardy side, to shout *'Oos that gutlord marching? Cut down on your porklife mate, get some exercise!'* at. We watched as one of them, a lean young thing with greasy brown hair, egged on his mate, an exercise in acne and red hair, to steal Lardy's wallet from his back pocket. Another distracted him, and Ginger dipped his fingers into his pocket. He'd got it halfway out when Lardy noticed, and, with a 'Bastards!', flicked his gas lighter and aimed for the redhead. A jet roared out: God knows what he'd done to it, but the flame was at least two feet. He missed Ginger, but managed to set light to the greasy haired one, singeing his quiff. They were all laughing their heads off as they did this, even as the lean young thing patted his hair out.
'The things we do for entertainment,' sighed Taylor, 'although I can't help feeling that he got what he deserved for egging the other on. Can you possibly imagine this happening anywhere else other than Britain? They're even laughing about it; Where else would you get people giggling about your friend nicking from you, then him roaring with joy as you set light to him?'
'It's all the fear thing again, isn't it? It's the way of coping with the fear – make it all a big joke.'
'I don't know. I think it's all about us lot generally being so buttoned up about everything, and the only real release we can find is in drinking way too much, then doing absolutely stupid things and laughing them off, even in the teeth of the next day's

hangover. Talking of which, that is what we are most certainly headed for tomorrow.'

'And speaking of that, it requires sleep, which requires a place to sleep, and I haven't asked you yet where you were going to stay overnight. I have a floor that is at your service. I may even have something comfortable to sleep on.'

' I thought you were never going to offer,' Taylor grinned. 'Thank you, I will certainly take you up on it.'

'How long were you planning on staying?' I asked, suddenly wondering whether I was going to see him again after this night. For some reason, I don't know, it came to mind that this was just a farewell from him, that after tonight he would disappear on his travels once more, and gradually fade from the memory like a photo left in the sunlight too long.

'I've got to be off in the morning – as you can see, I haven't come equipped for a particularly long stay.'

'But you'll be back?'

'Oh yeah, now I know you're here; then again, you might decide to get back on the road once more – then who knows? This is a very funky place, Dan,' he said, gesturing to the Turtle, 'but it isn't the be all and end all. You are not trapped, not at all. You can be free whether you choose to stay here or whether you decide to get moving again. It all depends on the reason you're going or staying - that has to be honest, otherwise there's no point. I ran until I found out that it was like trying to compete against a shadow self, the dark spot of ourselves we want to escape, that always and ever keeps pace with us and eventually will overtake us. Then when I'd worked that out, I realised I didn't have to run anymore. You're still trying to decide that.'

He took a deep swig of one of his beers and drained it, then let out a sudden enormous belch. 'Whatever, I'll be around: Maybe not close, but I'll be there, man. And, I daresay, so will Beattie.' He got out his fags and we lit up, then he punched my arm and grinned. 'Write to her Dan, write to her! You've got nothing to lose, except her saying 'no', and I don't think that's likely. Hell, look at us, we're in our thirties now, we're getting past it some might say; we needn't be scared of any fucker, we don't get freaked out by the idea of death any more,'

'Speak for yourself, I'm in no hurry to bloody die!' I said hastily.

'Neither am I,' continued Taylor, 'but die I will. I know that. But not today,' he grinned, 'not now, not fucking today!', and he laughed, a full, broad, gleeful laugh, one that defies the knowledge of decay and horror that time wrings out of us, a laugh that had its roots in the hunger for life. 'Come on, drink up, let's get really roaring pissed!'

Even if I'd had the desire to, I don't think I could have drunk any faster. I was feeling bloated and saggy, and I was already tanked up enough. I drank calmly, watching the scenes around me, watching for the signs in people's faces that talked of other things than what they wished to show. Having seen the fear that lurked everywhere in Bar Med, I wondered if it was possible to construct meanings by observing carefully and diligently enough. Places could clearly have meanings; for example, the Purple Turtle had once spoken of drunken joy, but Taylor's interpretation of the same phenomenon was, I was sure, something entirely different and exotic. I wanted to see with another's eyes, and see how what I perceived to be solid in one way would melt, reform and become the same thing, except replete with different significances, different meanings.

Of course, I was off my tits, but the whole game became fun. Seen one way, everyone was a fluid, writhing, excited mass; from another angle, laughing faces seemed more like tormented rictuses, everything was a symbol of anxiety, and the turning and moving of limbs in the crowd nothing more than the thrashing of bodies in agony, and this scene would melt once more, and become something more normal, more acceptable. Yet while these people before my very eyes underwent these strange transformations, while shadows of emotions danced across their visages, none seemed aware of the tremendous alterations they were capable of: and I realised that I, too, had undergone the same. I tried to communicate this marvellous fact to Taylor.

'I am most definitely pissed, Taylor,' I groaned suddenly, 'everything's going fuzzy and out of focus.'

'Good. That shows the booze is working.'

One tall figure came striding towards me. He had long flowing green hair and glasses, and was wearing a stripy South American – type top, combats and sandals. His face was world-weary and solid, and blue eyes peered through slightly puffy lids. He came

right up, looming over both of us, pointed one thick finger at me and said,
'Arse.'
'Well, I'll be damned! Mosey Hunt! How the fuck are you?'
'Not bad! How are you mate!' He roared, then took a drag of his cigarette; He had it clenched between the middle and ring fingers of his left hand, and clasped both his hands together as he took a drag through a hole he made between his thumbs. He grinned.
Mosey Hunt was yet another old school mate, although I had more time for him than many of the others. He had been commonly seen as the school eccentric, and his career ever since, what I'd heard about it, had only confirmed this. After being kicked out of his house by his parents when he was eighteen, he'd first taken revenge by trashing their entire kitchen, then he'd camped down by the river for the main part of a year. His appearance was always enthusiastic and colourful, to put it mildly. Green hair was relatively boring for him. He had an air that reminded me of some of the Saddhus I'd come across in India, and some of those who claimed to be dervishes when I'd crossed the middle east. Despite his exotic appearance, he'd never travelled extensively; rather, he was like Blakey at the Turk's, and did all his journeying inside his mind. It was widely believed that this was probably a more exciting place, considering Mosey's character and his willingness to experiment with all kinds of exotic herbs and spices.
 I introduced him to Taylor, who waved his hand lazily, which I took to mean that he was too drunk to bother impressing anyone.
'Taylor Coleridge. I know that name. Where from?' mused Mosey, but briefly. He looked Taylor up and down. 'We've met, I'm sure. But whatever. Come with me, I've got seats,' and he drifted serenely through the crowd, which seemed to part before him. He led us to the benches near the rear exit, and rapidly introduced us to several of his friends. I can't remember their names, now; I just recall there was one bald guy who somehow reminded me of a rabbit, another fat man who even in the heat was wearing a thick jumper, an incredibly beautiful woman with olive skin curled up on the bench and someone of indeterminate sex with close cropped black hair, very pale skin

and thin with it, dressed in dark baggy clothes and staring into space. After a flurry of introductions, he flopped down among them, his hair flapping into his face, with an air of world-worn tiredness. He looked out from under his brows, his eyes occasionally glinting like a flash of lightning seen between clouds from afar, and smoked his smoke between his cupped hands. Taylor stared at him, fascinated.
'Now this is very cool,' he said, trying to whisper in my ear above the roar of the crowd and the music, 'look at your man here. Notice his calmness, his supreme indifference to what goes on around him. What do you think he sees? How does he perceive this place around him? He's like some kind of Buddha, some wild saint.'
'Don't tell him that, you'll only inflate his ego,' I replied, but didn't really mean it, as he had impressed me too. Maybe it was just the booze, too many fags and not enough food, but Mosey seemed to possess the place – its calm focus among the wild fug. He'd certainly impressed Taylor, and that I knew to be a rare thing. Now Taylor approached him, glass in hand.
'You said you knew me. I'm trying to work out if we've met.' He grinned, and took another mouthful of dinner. I lit my fag, and watched what would happen between these two. 'Maybe we've passed each other abroad. You travelled much?'
Mosey lit another cigarette, took a drag between clasped hands. 'No, I don't travel, man – why do you need to travel when there's so much space in your head? You think the same, I can see that.'
Taylor leaned in closer. 'But what if you need to travel?'
'Do you need to? Why? What For? Travel is a lie; All you meet is exactly the same thing.'
'It depends what you're looking for, and why – you may meet the same, but you may look at the same with a different eye. What the tourist sees and the resident knows are different things and the same.'
They were sitting directly facing each other now, and smoking furiously. I had the impression of two kindred spirits facing off against each other. Suddenly, I felt extremely hot.
'Taylor, I'm getting some fresh air.'
'Sure, sure,' he said, not taking his eyes off Mosey, 'Mosey and I here are about to have an interesting conversation, I believe.'

I staggered through the garden doors, and stood at the head of the steps leading down. I gazed down at the heaving mass beneath me. I took a deep gulp of fresh air – although it was still humid, it was fresher than before – and looked up into the night sky. From what I could see of it, it was getting cloudy, and boded rain. Whichever way we played it, I reckoned we were going to get wet on our way back tonight. I looked back down on the crowd, but still the same tricks were being played on my mind – one minute, there was a normal crowd of people, the next, the crowd transformed itself into some hideous, writhing face, before recomposing itself.

'Come on, move back in or move down the stairs please,' said one of the bouncers to me, waving his hands in the general direction of the garden. I went down the steps, and joined the general melee of the garden crowd. Again, there was nowhere to sit, so I took up a place near the bar, and settled to watching what was going on around me. Despite already being crowded, more and more kept piling in, mainly to escape from the sheer heat of indoors. The two bouncers kept guard over the place, scanning for any signs of trouble, or chatting casually to each other, and occasionally guiding someone downwards. I first let my eyes wander casually wander over the crowd, inventing stories for the various people who caught my attention, stories that for all I knew were absurd or inherently true. My mind drifted through this in a happy alcoholic fug, picking up snatches of conversation that I added to the myth-making in my head. One thing I began to notice, however, was the seemingly extraordinary number of people with some kind of injury. I saw two people hopping around on crutches, one with an obviously broken leg, the other just kind of limping; Several people with their arms in slings or plaster; Another woman in a wheelchair, having a drinking competition with her mates; and a man with the most absurd amount of bandaging round his head, almost a turban, with a dark red stain on one side above his right ear. Then there were others with cuts, nicks, grazes and stitches, some of them clearly quite fresh. The strange thing was, or so it was to me, no one seemed to mind this vale of agony – instead, they were all cheerfully accepting of it all; even when the guy with the broken leg suddenly fell over, he joined in the laughter with everyone else. It crossed my mind that if this lot were in

Accident and Emergency, wielding their fresh wounds, rather than in a beer garden knocking back the ale, their whole demeanour and attitude would be different – 'tears instead of beers' was the refrain going through my head. Something Taylor had said earlier on came back to me, about location making a difference to attitude. It seemed I was getting an object example of the idea. Also, I couldn't get round why so many wounded were so happy; Then something else he'd said came back, and I realised I was focusing on one set of people rather than the mass. I changed my focus, and now those broken legs, arms and so on disappeared into the background. I saw one twentysomething girl, her arm in plaster, transform in front of me from one of the wounded, into just another reveller, then I reckoned she became a symbol for calm, then one for joy of living, then other symbolisms and meanings, each layered upon the other, a spiral of possibilities. This exercised my boozed-up head, and I understood that just by focusing my attention in any given way, I could make the world around me be something other than it was. The paranoia I'd felt earlier, when, walking down Friar Street, Reading had suddenly become sinister and exotic, now seemed absurd, and I thought now that I was in a playground of many faces, many mazes, many labyrinths. It seemed that a door that had been firmly shut in my mind had been not so much opened as kicked in by Taylor that day. Drunkenly ecstatic, I wanted to let him into this sudden revelation, this wonderful and terrible knowledge of what was right in front of my face, all our faces. I found that I couldn't move, though: Instead, I was stuck staring into a lit window in the building next door and the shadows moving inside. On the wall, which I now apprehended fully in its clarity, quiddity and consonance, seeing how each neat brick supported each other, how each part went to create the whole, There was a fire ladder, reduced to shadows in the night, and the shadows were replete with meaning. It was as if everything around me was shouting out messages in a joyous harmony. I just stood there, lost in wonder in a myriad of ideas, glinting with sudden light in the darkness. I believe I was shuddering with the shock of the sudden frenzy of thoughts rushing through me. All I could do was mouth 'wow.wow.wow.', looking like a goldfish, I would think.

Even now, thinking back to that night, I really don't understand it. It was as if the whole world had unfurled its strange musky flower, one full of mysteries, that's all I can say. Of course, one can't keep smelling the flower the same way: It would be impossible to function in this tired, venal world of ours if one did so. But once it has happened, then it becomes easier to see that the construction of meanings we place upon our quotidian existence is flimsy, no more and no thicker than a scene painting in the theatre – easy enough to tear away and see what lies beyond. It only needs the realisation that what we choose to see is not genuine. Anyway, I had promised to myself that I wouldn't interrupt my narrative, yet I felt the need to at this point. I'll let me continue.

The sensation seemed to go on for ages, but was probably no more than a couple of minutes; It faded slowly, a mental firework display gradually fading in the mind's night sky. It suddenly occurred to me that if the world could be seen like this, in the manifold ways that I had just experienced, then what the Fucking Weirdo had said earlier, about Taylor and I being inside an infernal narrative was, from his perspective at least, quite true. This freaked me out again, briefly, until I said to myself that my perspective must therefore be equally valid, and I vowed I wouldn't let his mad idea rattle me again. I took a deep breath, and let myself be enveloped by the real world again. Immediately, a coarse, choppy sea of voices and music rushed and lapped against me, and I was once more within something entirely comprehensible and, yes, mundane. I had, I don't know, dived beneath the surface, or reached into the sky, or whatever, but now I was skimming merrily on the surface of things. I felt the need for a piss, so I lumbered up the steps and back in. Taylor and Mosey were still talking vociferously, wagging and pointing their fingers at each other, leaning towards each other to make a point. It was too loud to make out what they were saying, but I had the feeling it was something that not even those sat next to them could make head nor tail of. If the music and noise and chatter had suddenly died down to nothing and the whole world had stopped to listen to them, still they would have been incomprehensible, it seemed to me;

they were talking in Enochian, and their conversation was not for others. I caught Taylor's eye, and motioned that I was going to the pisser. I slid through the crowds, trudged up the stairs under the watchful eyes of the Star Trek posters and into the bog. In the brushed steel wall, as I pissed, I caught sight of myself. I seemed older than I was, all droopy eyes, receding hair and sagging face, and I wondered if that was the face other people saw when they looked at me. Then I considered that it was just a face, and therefore not that much.

When I got back to the bar, Taylor was sat alone, arms stretched along the bench, head pointed to the ceiling, smoking serenely.

'Where's Mosey?' I asked, sitting down next to him.

'Gone, along with his entourage, obviously,' he replied. 'He said something about going somewhere else – some posh bar. He said he wouldn't get in, but he might have some fun taunting the doormen.'

'What were you two talking about? You were at it hammer and tongs.'

'Oh, this and that, this and that. Metaphysical stuff. It doesn't matter now.'

He continued to puff on his fag.

'Come on,' he said, suddenly getting to his feet and swaying, 'you haven't shown me the garden. And you were right – it's sweltering in here.'

We went into the garden, but where it had exploded with weirdness earlier, now it remained stubbornly the same. The breeze was picking up slowly, and the scent that comes before a storm increased. As we got a couple of vodkas from the bar, I tried, and failed dismally, to explain what had happened to me earlier on. Though I had a clear sensation in my head of what had occurred, it seemed to evade language. Taylor listened to me, head on one side, and smiled.

'You haven't been trying any special herbs, have you? Seriously, I think I know what you mean – I think. It could have been some kind of epiphany, some revelation, but if it is, then it's yours, you know?'

'But it's like there's a light on in my head. Taylor, and you turned it on somehow.'

'Well, thank you for the compliment, but it's your head, your light. Maybe I just showed you where the switch was.'
We got our drinks. Taylor said, 'so, you still trapped here? Are you still going to escape?'
'No. And yes. Or maybe that's the other way round. I think I have some exploring to do in my own head.'
'That's the spirit. Talking of exploration, where does that lead?' He was pointing towards the side of the building, where a stream of people were going back and forth.
'That goes to the cellar bar, you know, the dance section?'
'Let's take a look.'
So we wandered round the corner into the cellar bar. If anything, it was even hotter and more humid than the main bar. The darkness was lightened by only a few coloured lights on what passed for the dance floor. A few people were dancing, and they were all clearly off their heads. One woman, who I took to be in her forties, with a large mane of curled hair and t-shirt and leggings that were far too tight for her was lolling around, a bottle of Smirnoff ice held loosely in her hand. There was a couple, frantically crushed up against each other, and a few blokes waving and whooping to the beat of some dance song from the early nineties. As in Bar Med, there were clusters of people, mostly men, on the purlieus of the dance floor, watching what was going on. There was a palpable difference in the atmosphere here, however; where in the other place it had been an avid, hungering kind of stare that was prevalent, here it was more resigned and accepting. Taylor and I stood around a high table in silence, vaguely observing the comings and goings of those around us once more. Opposite me there was a dark alcove, with several figures lounging inside. Although I couldn't hear them, I could see that they were chatting languidly about something or other. One of them was incredibly fat – I mean a real bloater. He sat and puffed and sweated, and looked like he couldn't even move. Another of them produced a note, a tenner or a fiver, from a pocket, and holding it up to a light, was explaining something about it to his friend, who also took it and examined it. The one who produced the note was scratching extravagantly, rummaging now in his armpit, then in his head, and after that his legs, then back to his armpit again. He was doing it so much that he was obviously making others in the

alcove feel the same, and they were having unobtrusive scratches, too.
'Keep watching them, and you'll end up with an itch too,' said Taylor in my ear. 'I prefer to watch the dance floor.'
I turned my attention back to that, although there wasn't really anything worth seeing, apart from one idiot who kept running backwards and forwards, yelling, first to the amusement of others, then to indifference.
'What's the time?' I asked Taylor.
'Just about one,' he said. 'Are we staying? I think a walk might do some good right now. Is there anywhere else open?'
'Pretty much all of Friar Street – they'll be going until two.'
'Come on, let's have a look.'
'They're all, you know, so-called upmarket – No Trainers, and arseholes fighting type places.'
'Oh, come on – let me see a real Reading Nightclub.'
'Alright then.'
We drained our vodkas, and made our by now woozy way to the stairs, up and out into the night. A few large, heavy drops of rain spattered here and there.
'We're going to get wet tonight, I think.'
'Who cares? It'll sober us up.'
'Right, this way, then.'
And we walked back up Union Street towards the centre of town.

Twenty Two: Through a child's eyes

My Friend the Angel climb'd up from his station into the mill; I remain'd alone, & then this appearance was no more, but I found myself sitting on a pleasant bank beside a river by the moonlight, hearing a harper who sung to the harp:
William Blake

In which the Author, sensing that the end of the story is not too far off now, makes his final interruption to the text before becoming entirely immersed in it, much to the relief of the reader.

Imagine how you were when you were small, sitting in the back of the car on a long and tedious journey, you traced the course of a single cloud against a blue sky; imagine that that cloud could somehow remain impervious, and one day, years later, you see the same thing, again from the back of a car; what is the difference in the way you see it? Do you experience the same feelings, emotions, ideas? Again, picture a fairly distant relative you meet when you are five but then don't see again until you are twenty; what changes? Or you are taken to a park by your parents, and they take a photograph of you sat astride a statue of a recumbent lion that guards the playground area; In the photograph, the lion is enormous. Then many years pass, and you return with your own child, promising to the kid that there is a big, big, lion there, but when you arrive, there is only this rather tatty statue that is no more than knee high to you; What has happened?

What I'm trying to point out in my own clumsy way is that change, when it comes, happens to us as much as it happens to the outside world. The difference is, the alteration that occurs internally, that of the character, is often unnoticeable. The same, of course, occurs in the external world, where gradual, organic change is the norm. When Dan first returned from his travels, for example, he was somewhat surprised by the differences he could see in his home town, whereas his family, who'd stayed there all the time, had not registered the change. The internal landscape of the mind not only alters, it is unreliable, as unreliable as I have been on this little journey.

Perhaps it would be better if we could keep that sense of wonderment we all have as children, that the world remains a place of continual surprise; then the mundanities we have to deal with each day, the grind of things that weary us, oppress our bodies and minds, would become a little more tolerable. But of course, the world we accept as real won't let us do that – on the contrary, it expects us to have sensibilities and emotions and a sense of curiosity about as finely attuned as a brick. Either you learn to filter out the wondrous, the marvellous, the awesome and the terrible that pervade the everyday, or you sink under the weight of trying to live through it all. Only those for whom society has no use – the very young, the very old, those too ill and those who are certain to die – are allowed to peer through what is and see beyond.

I can see the end of this particular story appearing now; it is still on the horizon, but now it's becoming increasingly attainable. Of course, the story will continue, just as it had a prelude; who can truly say where stories begin and end. Think of all the characters that have appeared – what about their stories? Where do they go? Do you think I will just dismantle them, leave them in the darkness where the light of narrative does not shine? To be honest, I think it's rather beyond my capabilities now. While I haven't appeared in the story for the best part of a few pages, I have been present – how couldn't I? – making a record of what was going on. It's a good job that the Purple Turtle was crowded, that's all I can say. And now I go to, as it were, put on the greasepaint and slap and motley for my final appearance in the story. After that, I don't know whether you will hear from me again – but then, I've never really known, caught as I am in this book's capricious whims. I hope, however, that I have not been too tedious a companion to you, as you have wandered down the road with me; Maybe you have even profited from what I have said; perhaps I have made you consider what you are reading, and how you read it; I sincerely hope I have been a good guide to Reading

Right, Show Time!

Twenty-three: Giants and Ice
An eye for an eye leaves the whole world blind.

Gandhi

Our intrepid topers reach almost the last stage of their day long stagger round Reading town centre; they witness policemen and fighting and the breakdown of the night; they enter a club for one last drink, and encounter the Weirdo.

For one o'clock in the morning, Broad Street was remarkably busy. Gangs of young people roamed and swaggered along it; one girl was vomiting copiously outside Ann Summers; three boys were pissing on Carphone Warehouse, while some more were having a fight; and all the while, a ridiculously merry pipe tune was being played by none other than the piper from Duke Street Bridge. A few people were even capering merrily in front of him and his dog. And from near and far there was a muted roar of thousands, spilling from and staggering to different pubs, clubs and bars, via the kebab shop or a doorway for a quick slash. Sometimes, there was a shout or a yell or a sudden shriek nearby, or laughter clattering off the stores and shops, but mostly there was this growling – the throat of the Friday night mob. It wasn't the friendly, happy sound from earlier, rather it had a note of menace, of ugly threat to it. And it was continuous, like the rumble of traffic on a busy road heard from afar. It would only be when the last bar had closed, the last kebab shop had served the last kebab, the last bus had run and the last taxi had picked up the last reveller, that it would become muted and sleep until Saturday evening came around.

We crossed the street and entered Victoria Street, heading towards the station. At the Friar Street junction, there were two police vans, their lights flashing, and several police busy with something in the road.

'I wonder what's happened,' said Taylor.

'Oh, that. That's the usual Friday night routine. They start cordoning off some of the streets to persuade people out of the town centre.'

'Do they actually need so many cops?'

'Yes. It gets lively, shall we say. Especially when you have two gangs in fancy dress squaring up to each other.'

'Talking of which...'

And there, ahead of us, were two guys, or at least I presumed they were two guys dressed up. They were wearing what I can only call giant costumes – large platform soles, some kind of foam rubber outfit that made them ridiculously fat, and foam rubber head and shoulders. They were swinging rubber clubs at each other and at passersby, and roaring. They were being egged on by their more normally dressed friends, who were also dragging along another giant, who was wrapped in plastic chains. A couple of police were smiling, but keeping a wary eye on them. Three girls in fairy outfits tripped by, and got the foam rubber club treatment, making them squeal and laugh. We were edging by, smiling, when one of them saw us and shook his club. He said something, but it was unintelligible because of his costume.

'Sorry mate, what did you say?' I said, laughing.

'He said, 'what's the password?'' said the other, waving his club.

'I dunno. Please?'

Taylor looked at the second giant, suddenly laughing his head off.

'Nice costume, that – it suits you. Where did you get this finery from?'

The first giant gave a muffle reply, then the second interjected, 'you know, from the costume store in Caversham road? Good, isn't it?'

'Yeah, I like that, I'll have to get the same one of these days. Have a nice evening,' said Taylor, and we both sauntered past without being clobbered.

'Chat to them nicely, and they'll always let you pass,' Taylor mused.

'Who are They?'

'You know. Them. Those who stand in your way. Them.'

'I suspect, Taylor, that you may have had enough booze for one night.'

'I suspect, Dan, that you may be correct. However, there are still places open and drinks to drink. Where are we going?' He peered up Friar Street. The raindrops slowly increased in size and intensity, and there was a distant growl of thunder.

'You choose, man. It's all yours.'
'Then let's fall in the first one we come across – this is it.'
We stood outside a neon-lit sign, swish glass doors and enormous bouncers.
'The Ice Bar. Ice. Coolness. That'll do us. Come on.'
We went past the bouncers, who gave us no more than a cursory glance, satisfied, it would seem, with our state of sartorial elegance, and into a raving pit of madness – it was seething, noisy and humid – hardly the well of coolness Taylor had been expecting, I suspected, judging from the disappointed look on his face. There was some kind of breeze, from a faulty air conditioner I guessed, that sent intermittent waves of cool air gusting towards us; However, it was hardly effective, except in sending a wave of sweat, ale and fag odours our way. Taylor pushed and elbowed his way to the bar and ordered us something cold in bottles.
'There you go. That's about as cold as it's going to get tonight, I think.'
'Cheers. Shall we call it a night after this?'
'Yeah, I think so. The beer really has started to get to me. Man, I will crash out tonight!'
We wandered towards the dance floor, looking for somewhere to sit or at least lean against. All around us, there were people in a similar condition or worse; gangs and couples slumped against each other, or tottered back and forth; scuffles broke out here and there – not enough for the bouncers to get involved, but enough to add a frisson of tension to the already palpitating atmosphere. People were skidding in puddles of spilt drink or worse. The whole evening now seemed bereft of any lingering joy, as though it had gradually leached from the scene. Far from the happy, relaxed faces of earlier, this lot seemed, if not unhappy, then grimly determined to enjoy themselves and stay dancing until closing time. For them, I could see, enjoyment meant drinking too much and coming into town, and hanging on for as long as possible, before dragging oneself back home and sleeping for the rest of the weekend. Of course, I was no exception, and I realised I probably wouldn't be surfacing much before lunchtime the next day.
Taylor was looking at me as if he could read my thoughts. He smiled, and nodded his head at the grimly determined dancers.

'They're in a prison, but can't even see it. You were too, until an hour ago. Now your eyes are opened. These will have to wait for their own epiphanies, though I doubt it will occur for the vast majority of them, mainly because they don't want it to happen – too scary, for most.'

'Yeah, but it depends what they really want and what they need, doesn't it?'

'They're told what it is they want, and instructed to ignore what it is they need. But sometimes, when you do get what you want, you dimly begin to see what it is that you actually need – it's hard, but you can get there.'

I wasn't entirely sure I followed what he meant, but I nodded my head sagely, for the look of the thing. It was highly unlikely that either of us could have made any sense at that time of night, anyway. And anyway, what on earth could possibly make any sense at nearly two in the morning? Yes, I'd had many late-night conversations in which we'd solved the problems of the world, but by the morning, those ideas had dissolved, as evanescent and as booze fumes. It occurred to me that my heart was no longer in this evening, and I was about to suggest that we knock the beers back and head home, when who should I see but the Fucking Weirdo. I was certain it was him, even though he was dressed in better clothes than I had seen him earlier, and his hair was neatly slicked back. He looked directly at me, smirked, and beckoned me to follow him.

'Taylor, it's him! Over there, look! The Fucking Weirdo! He wants us to follow him.'

Taylor watched him, then said, 'Not us, you. He's asking you to come. Better go and see what it is he wants.'

'Come on man, he's been bugging us all evening. Let's go over and sort him out.'

' You don't need me to do that. I'm just going to sway here for a bit. Go get him.'

I strode through the crowd towards where I'd seen him, then saw him sat in a dark corner, his legs on the table in front of him, smoking a cigarette. He was dressed entirely in black now, and nothing scruffy; rather, it looked to my jaded and drunken eye like expensive designer gear.

He blew a smoke ring, and said, 'Do you believe me now?'

'Believe what?' I asked, confused.

'That you are in Hell.'
'Don't talk bollocks. Now tell me, what the fuck are you doing following us around?'
'Following you? Why should I follow you when you've been following my agenda all night?'
'What?'
He took another puff of his cigarette, then abruptly stubbed it out.
'You are in Hell,' he repeated, 'and you are merely a character in a piece of fiction. You have no sentient life of your own, but are rather a mouthpiece for the Author's wishes, whims, ideas, aspirations and frustrations. You are a writer's plaything, nothing more. Sit down.'
I was sitting down, facing him. How I came to be seated from my previous standing position, and how a chair actually seemed to have come from nowhere for me to sit on in the first place, I have no idea; However, I was very pissed, so it's entirely possible I just collapsed on it without noticing.
'No, it's not possible,' he said.
'What's not?'
'What you just thought. You're sitting there because I want you to sit there.'
'Look, I don't know which planet you've dropped off, but will you stop with the stupid fucking mind games?'
'I'm not playing games, Dan. Well, I am, actually. It's tremendous fun.'
'Who the fuck are you?' I said slowly, vehemently.
'What I said earlier, when you and Taylor laughed at me. I am The Author. I am writing about you and your little drinking tour of Reading. I just thought it was high time we were introduced properly.'
Now I just did not know what to think. All I could do was look at him incredulously. He had to be mad, just had to. On the other hand, the heebie jeebies he'd put on me earlier returned. I must have shifted uncomfortably, because he said, smirking,
'What's the matter? Have your heebie jeebies of earlier returned?'
'No, I'm trying to make up my mind whether to deck you or not, you weird twat.'

'Even if you tried, you wouldn't be able to land a punch,' he snarled, suddenly vicious. 'Even if you tried, it wouldn't happen because I'm in control of the narrative. The thought, if I so chose to, wouldn't even cross your mind. It's only doing so because I thought it'd be more interesting in terms of the story.'
'You, my friend, are so full of shit, you know that?'
He looked up to the ceiling, then said,
'Daniel Thompson, aged 35, born and bred in Reading. Goes travelling in 1994, travels across the world. Meets his good friend, Taylor Coleridge, age 35 – and I know you don't know his real age, but I do, in Delhi, India, in 1999. They travel together through India, then around the Gulf, the Arabian Peninsula, and up the Red Sea. They are separated in Beirut; you continue your travels alone, meeting the lovely Beatrice Porti in late 2000. You fail to get it on with her for reasons best known to yourself, and are currently debating whether you should get back in contact with her or not, your only hesitation being engendered by fear of rejection. You return to Reading in early 2004, and have been at a loose end ever since. You are anxious and depressed, and the arrival of your old friend comes as a ray of light between dark clouds. How am I doing so far? Do you realise, by the way, how stupid you look?'
And he smiled at my very obvious discomfiture. How the fuck had he known all that?
'So I've got a stalker,' I said slowly, with rising anger thickening my throat. 'all that you could have found out anywhere.'
'Really? Recognise this?'
He pulled out of his pocket a couple of beer mats and a piece of card ripped from the back of a fag packet, covered in a rough map. It was the map we'd drawn in the Hope Tap earlier, showing the route we'd taken up until then. I saw my scrawls and Taylor's confident, neat handwriting. The Weirdo had somehow attached the pieces, and had drawn in, in red ink, our subsequent route. I thought Taylor had put the map in his pocket when we left the Hope.
'How come I've got this then?'
'You could easily have picked that up, ' I replied.
'I didn't need to pick it up! I had it already, in here,' he said, tapping his head. 'Besides, if you want to play this logically, you two drew this after I'd been thrown out of the pub.'

'Nothing to stop you going back though.'
'Is that really feasible?'
'More feasible than you ranting on about us being fictional characters in some piece of work.'
He sighed. 'What will it take to convince you that you are not real, and that I am who I say I am, namely your creator?'
' Don't give me that omnipotent shit. You're just a cracked-up FUCKING WEIRDO.'
'Oh, I do wish I hadn't made you swear like that.'
'Shut the fuck up! Shut up! All I am doing, right, is having a pleasant time with my mate Taylor. That's all. I am not being governed, ruled or manipulated by anyone, least of all you. And there's nothing, nothing at all that you can do to convince me that we're part of your story, right?'

He tossed a book across the table. It was The Divine Comedy, part one.

'Open it up,' he said, casually. 'Read the plot outline on the first page.'

I opened it. A date, set a few months back, faced me. Underneath it was scrawled, 'Dante. Dan T? Poet – Coleridge? Pub Crawl – meet famous people – discussions about reality. Who? Related to Reading! Blake, Wilde, Bryan Adams???!!! Jane Austen?? – start in Emmer Green, go over Reading Bridge, then to these pubs..'

And he had listed the pubs we had been to that night, ending with the Ice Bar. Beside each bar, he'd written notes, explaining its relationship to Hell and the punishments. As I was reading through these, he pulled out his tattered notebook, and slung it over to me as well.

'Have a leaf through that, while you're about it,' he said, and yawned.

I flicked through it; it seemed to consist of lots of different things – bus tickets, a menu for a kebab shop, a transcript for some texting, a diary entry, other things, a lots of scribbled notes and ideas. I read hard when I came to:

You are in Hell,' he repeated, 'and you are merely a character in a piece of fiction. You have no sentient life of your own, but are rather a mouthpiece for the Author's wishes, whims, ideas,

aspirations and frustrations. You are a writer's plaything, nothing more. Sit down.'
'No, it's not possible,' he said.
'What's not?'
'What you just thought. You're sitting there because I want you to sit there.'
'Look, I don't know which planet you've dropped off, but will you stop with the stupid fucking mind games?'
'I'm not playing games, Dan. Well, I am, actually. It's tremendous fun.'

'Do you see?' he said, and smiled triumphantly at the look of drunken shock on my face.
'That's bullshit, man, and you're full of it!'
'No, I'm not. I'm just trying to prove to you that I am sincere, and that this really is merely a story.'
'Why, do you get a kick out of it, or something? This proves nothing, absolutely nothing. You could easily have memorised these lines.'
He became visibly angry.
'What am I going to have to do. I'll tell you what, I'm going to stop writing right now. I am going to make myself some food, and you are going to have to stay like this until I get back.'
He clicked his fingers.

Nothing happened.

'Well, that was successful,' I said.

'I stopped writing! I did,' he exclaimed. A thought began to gleam in my mind.

'If this is a story,' I replied, speaking slowly, 'Then surely it has certain functions and rules, yes?'

'Of course,' he snapped. 'a narrative isn't a narrative otherwise; it would just be randomly happening things – what's happened to you today should surely prove to you that what you are experiencing is not real.'

' What I mean is, that there are rules like gravity and so forth. Conventions, shit like that.'

'Yes.'

'If that is the case, how can I possibly understand what is going on outside the story? It's beyond my personal frame of reference - I don't even have the faculties to even perceive that there is anything beyond what I can comprehend.'

'What's your point?', he barked, suddenly twisting uneasily in his chair.

'That there is no way on Earth that you can prove to me that you are what you say you are. There is no way within the conventions that it can be demonstrated, is there?'

He was silent and, I thought, somewhat worried looking. I was on a roll. A big, fat, booze-inspired roll.

'You say that you are the Author, and that we are in Hell. Well, I say bollocks to that. By my conventions, you are nothing more than a Fucking Weirdo and for all I know, I'm in Heaven, but I do know that in this, present, real world, I am in Reading, I am deeply drunk, I am with my friend, and that this and this,' I waved his books at him, 'are worth bugger all. I reckon you've been making it up as you go along, probably because you are a sad little friendless sack of crap. Now would you please fuck off and die somewhere?'

'You – you cannot talk to me like that! I created you!' he stood up, angry and upset, and I realised he was dressed just as before, except he'd tidied himself up a bit. 'I'll kill you off! That'll make you see!'

'How, exactly?' It was my turn to smile and put my feet up. 'How would I notice if I no longer exist?'

He was clearly foxed.
'What are you going to do then, Author? Screw it up and start all over again? Wouldn't that defeat the object?'
'I could if I wanted to,' he replied, nervously.
'Something else strikes me. If, as you say, I am a character in your story, then it means you must be as well.'
'Yes, that's true.'
'In that case, if this is a narrative with set boundaries and conventions, you are also bound by them – you can't just go out to break your own tale, it wouldn't make any sense.'
'Don't you try that on me! I'll do what I please with my story!'
'Go ahead, it won't make a difference – but I don't think you can.' And I laughed at the weirdy fucker. He just stood up and stayed there, balling his fists and moving nervously on his feet.
'What are you going to do now, weirdo? Punch me? Come on then – you don't have anything I'm afraid of, twat!'
And he did! He swung for me! He started lashing out, fists and feet flailing wildly and fortunately missing me. I stood up and pushed him back, roughly. He came at me again, snarling almost incomprehensibly 'You – you upstart – piece of crap character – should have made you die in agony – cancer – wear this!' and he swung at me, this time lamping me in the shoulder, which only made me sway a bit more than I was already doing. I pushed him back and before he came on again, three very large bouncers were manhandling him to the floor and Taylor appeared at my side.
'Have you been upsetting him?' he asked mildly.
'Only a little.'
One of the bouncers looked at me.
'You all right mate? What happened? Do you know this bloke?'
'I'm fine – he's just some twat, I don't really know who he is. One minute he's talking to me, the next he goes thug.'
The bouncers pulled him onto his feet, and held him tightly, and he began shouting his head off.
'You miserable little fuckers! Let me go – I am your Author! I am writing about you! You're fucking fictional, all of you! Let me go, or I'll give you all cancer and tiny cocks in my story, you hairy-arsed cocksuckers!'
'Yeah, yeah, I'll give you 'Author', mate,' growled one of the bouncers, and they dragged him away, screaming and cursing.

I picked up the two books and the map, which had been left on the table.

'What're those?' asked Taylor.

'Oh, they belong to him. You can have a read later, for amusement value. This map's ours – he must have picked it up in the Hope.'

'Thought I'd put it in my pocket. Never mind.'

As we talked, the lights went up. The revels were at an end.

'Time to get going, I think,' I said.

'I agree. Shall we kebab?'

'Sounds good to me. Soak up a bit of the booze.'

'Damn right.'

So we sauntered out into Station Road with the rest of the chattering, drifting crowd. It was raining in earnest now, a welcome breath of freshness after so much humidity; thunder rumbled off the buildings and lightning briefly punctured the darkness. The rain quickly broke the crowds, who scattered this way and that for bus shelters, kebab shops and taxi ranks, while discarded wrappers, cartons and flyers for promotions drifted and dissolved in the watery road. Policemen waited silently in rows ushering people homeward and away from the centre; a police car went by lazily, slowly cruising with its light flashing towards the statue of Edward the Seventh, then round towards the Apex Plaza. We trudged slowly, looking out for a kebab shop that wasn't packed. The one in Station Road was full, partly with people escaping the weather; the same went for the shops in Station Hill. The murmurous, many-mouthed creature called the mob was slowly quietening down now, softening from a growl to a echoing, choppy sea of sound, pierced here and there by a shout or a laugh or sobbing. We passed the queue of punters waiting for taxis outside the Station: Every few seconds, a black cab would be filled, whisk its clients away, and be replaced by another black cab. The taxis themselves were queued all the way down the hill, and their drivers were leaning on the bodywork of their machines, sharing a joke and a laugh before it was their turn to move forward and gather their next fare. I looked at the faces and postures of those who were waiting, and could easily read how they had perceived their night; A group of girls, still excited and giggling over someone called Steve; three lads, one of them dead drunk, scowling; a couple

with their backs turned to each other; a solitary man, looking up at the sky, then down at his feet, his shoulders hunched in anxiety; another man, his arms around two women, all of them laughing. Their stories seemed so obvious, so easy to read. I wondered whether mine had been as easy to see as well, and, considering the Weirdo, decided it must have been so.
'Are we getting a taxi?' Taylor asked.
'Let's walk. I can survive the rain.'
'Where are we getting our kebab then?'
'There's the Marmara in Caversham Road. It's a bit of a walk, but I want to sober up a bit.'
We walked down the hill, past the station and the buses, past the abandoned bus depot with the tatty old Mecca Bingo building on top, past the Malthouse, its windows dark except for a solitary top floor light gleaming, and past the office blocks and abandoned terrace of houses. Taylor got out his pack of fags, passed one to me and sparked up himself.
'So what we you talking about?'
'What was what talking about?'
'You and the Weirdo.'
'Oh, that.' And I related what he'd said to me and what I'd said to him and how he'd tried to deck me. Taylor grinned.
'Never a dull moment here, is it? We meet philosophers, pundits, drunks and giants, and now you meet a stalker who claims to be our God.'
'He didn't say that.'
'Yeah, but that's what he in effect meant. If he was saying that you and I are just characters in his story, then he is, effectively, the Creator.'
'Or the Devil.'
'Or the devil, yes. Interesting idea.'
'I wonder what's happening to him right now?'
'Unpleasant things involving those bouncers, I reckon.'
We turned the corner into Caversham road. People were still spilling out of the night club under the railway arches. The rain was getting a little lighter, but we decided to wait it out a bit underneath the bridge. A late night train rumbled slowly overhead, disturbing a pigeon from its roost. It dipped from its perch and flapped in three weary beats to the other side.

'Has it not occurred to you that he might have been telling the truth?'

'Well, it did, and he had me freaked out for a bit, but it's hardly likely, is it? and, to be quite frank, I'd be seriously pissed off to find out that God's some geek like the Fucking Weirdo was.'

'It's always possible that we are just characters in some great story,' said Taylor, spreading out his arms. 'All this is just some kind of dream, or some sort of joke.'

'Yeah, but that means everything is predestined then, doesn't it? It doesn't matter what the fuck I do, because whatever I do has already been determined. And that, I think, is bollocks.'

'How do you know you weren't destined to say that very thing?'

'Oh balls to it, Taylor. It's too bloody late for metaphysics.'

We both laughed, smoked our fags, and watched a couple of women in very short skirts and very high heels totter damply through the rain towards Caversham, holding their handbags over their heads for cover.

'Come on, let's get a bit more wet,' I said, and we followed on in their wake.

Twenty-four: Climbing up the hill to bed
Merrily, merrily, merrily, merrily, life is but a dream.

Our two sozzled chums trudge damply along the road; they enjoy a kebab; they walk slowly towards Caversham and then to Emmer Green; the story winds to its conclusion.

It was now getting on for half past two in the morning. A few cars passed us a we walked slowly and unsteadily up the road. We crossed over by the post office depot, where we could see night shift workers having a coffee break in the canteen. Outside Drews there was a kebab van, but I persuaded Taylor that it wasn't worth it – too much risk of it being cat in the pita bread. One man in a torn and bloody shirt had purchased something from there, and was leaning against the service hatch, helping himself to extra ketchup and chilli sauce, most of which was going down his arm. He finally managed to lift his sodden pocket of pita bread to his mouth, and promptly spilt half its contents down himself, although he was far too drunk to notice.
'Imagine when he wakes up in the morning to find his chest stained with meat and chilli,' I said. 'He probably won't have a clue about what happened to him at all. He'll have to invent something to tell his mates.'
'Well, we've all done the same kind of thing, I daresay. Don't you remember the first time you got blind drunk?'
'No, I don't. I was blind drunk. I know what you mean, though. I do recall there was this one guy I was at college with. He woke up one morning after a night on the lash to find himself fully clothed. As he took his jeans off, he discovered there was puke inside them.'
'Oh Jesus! How'd he managed that?' Taylor laughed.
'Well, he was puzzling it over for most of the day, but he reckoned it must have happened like this; he'd come in roaring drunk, and needed a dump, so he was sat on the bog, threw up in his trousers, and was so pissed that he just pulled them back on and went to bed.'

'That, or someone came along and filled his pants with puke. Interesting, isn't it, especially in the light of what's gone on today. If we're not sure of the facts, we make up the story that seems most reasonable and logical – we take what facts we do know and bend them to fit what we can only guess at.'

'I suppose so – it's like when people first saw the stars in the sky,' and here I looked up at the rain, which was becoming drizzle, 'they guessed that what they saw was a vast bowl with lights shining into it from outside, and then they wondered what could be outside, and they speculated about a vague idea called Heaven.'

We walked past the roundabout and Carter's. Caversham Road lay straight ahead of us, empty except for one car disappearing in the distance, and a few people hanging around outside Marmara Kebab. The poplars that lined the street cast damp shadows and broken orange light from streetlamps across the buildings, and whispered and rustled between themselves on the light breeze.

'Heaven, a vague idea,' mused Taylor. 'You're spot on there. Paradise is always vague – no one's got a single bloody clue what it's like. It always involves clouds and fluffiness and abstract happiness. I suspect that puppies and kittens may be involved somewhere along the line. Got absolutely nothing to do with bugger all. But the other side, well, that's easy. Hell is a piece of piss to evoke – burning, pain, torment, all in a variety of imaginative and fun ways.'

'Says a lot about people, that,' I replied, 'it suggests that the basic human condition is one of misery, sadism, cruelty and brutality.'

'For a lot of poor sods in this world, though, that's true – we've both seen it.'

'You're not far wrong there.'

We reached Marmara Kebab. There was a small queue, so we slumped into a couple of plastic chairs shackled to a table. I looked blearily along the brightly-lit menu panel. Photos that bore no true resemblance to what I was about to purchase vied for my attention; plump-looking shish kebabs with fresh salad, a hunk of roast chicken, a beautifully-presented succulent doner kebab in a fresh pita bread.

'Can I look at those books?'

'Sure.' I handed the Weirdo's copy of the Inferno and his notebook over, along with our map. 'What do you want?'
'Kebab's fine. And something to drink.'
I joined in the queue while Taylor flicked through the pages. The Turkish bloke behind the counter worked swiftly and efficiently, handling each customer with silent courtesy. He was obviously just counting down the minutes until he could jack it in for the night and get home. I wondered about how often he had to deal with pissed-up abuse from the punters; probably every Friday and Saturday night. His monosyllabic conversation was his best defence against foul-mouthed idiots at two in the morning. That and his large kebab sword. I put in our order and paid.
'Hold on a minute, mate, I'm gonna get some more salad and stuff. You wait there, yeah, I'll shout when it's ready.'
'OK.'
I went and sat back down. Taylor was still flicking through the books.
'Interesting, this,' he said, pushing it my way again, 'mad as a haddock, but interesting. I can see why he might have wanted you to think as though he was in control. Looks to me like he actually did have a story about someone on a pub crawl, and then we come along and hey presto, we fit the bill, more or less. Looks like he's added an awful lot today, as well. Look, he's used the same pen all the way from here to here. And it's the same in the front of this book too.'
He showed me the scrawls side by side.
'He could have had the pen for a while.'
'A felt tip? I don't think so. No, I reckon he's had this idea in his head for a while, then he and we coincide, he scrawls all this shit down in a fever of excitement, then shows it to you to try and convince you of what he was. Could be that the poor bastard is a bit dolalley as well.'
'A bit? He wasn't just off his trolley, he was out of the supermarket!'
'Whatever. I'll tell you something though, there are some interesting bits and pieces here, and he must have been stalking us a lot more carefully than we realised. He's obviously tracked us all through town - he's even scribbled down some stuff we were talking about. Weird.'

He pushed the books back over to me, and combed his hands through his hair. He looked wearily out into the night.
'It's been a long one today,' he said. 'Long, but good. What time is it?'
'Coming up for three, I think.'
'Not long before it's sunrise, then.'
The guy at the counter produced our food, we gathered it and went out. It had stopped raining completely, and the street was deserted and silent except for the gentle drip of water from the trees. We walked towards Caversham Bridge in silence, chewing on our doners. The sky above had cleared, and the stars gleamed through the freshened air. Far off our right, towards London, there was the odd flash of light as the thunderstorm headed east. We crossed at the traffic lights, and carried on to the bridge. Once we were on it, Taylor stopped in front of a granite plaque and read it with interest. It told of the old chapel that had existed on this side of the bridge in medieval times, and to which, according to the inscription, 'an oone-winged angel did bring the spere that perced our saviour's side'.
'Jesus! The Spear Of Destiny was brought to Reading?' he exclaimed, genuinely surprised.
'Apparently,' I said. I had heard of the story, but had never really given it much thought.
'Well, you live and learn. Imagine that, Dan – something that connected people here directly to what they believed in was here, on this spot. Just when you think everything is solid and comfortable and real – and you cannot get more real than trudging home at some godforsaken hour in the morning – you get reminded that there is the miraculous everywhere, all the time. Imagine what our Weirdo friend would say about us encountering this.'
'Yeah, I guess so. Now you mention it, that is a strange description. Why an angel with one wing? Was it limping or something?'
'Who knows? It's how someone saw it as being, and the same person probably genuinely believed that it was the spear carried by Longinus, and that it had slid into Christ's flesh. Whether it was actually true or not doesn't matter – faith made it real and relevant to that person.'

'So by the Weirdo's point of view, we are still his fictional characters – that's his faith, then.'

'If he wants to believe that, the yes, I suppose so, but the thing is that he's competing against other faiths and beliefs – ours that we actually exist, for example. And while he does that, he can't win. So balls to him.'

'What do you reckon it was like, this Spear Of Destiny?'

'Probably the same as all the others that wandered from palace to palace in Europe, I'd say; Old Roman spears must have been ten a penny in the middle east. But if you imagine all those pilgrims coming here, focusing the same thoughts and hopes on this precious, wonderful relic – well, I suspect that we'd have believed it was the real thing, as well.'

We carried on walking over the bridge. Beneath us, the Thames flowed darkly eastwards, its surface rippled by the breeze and dappled by the white shapes of swans floating here and there. We stopped again on the viewing platform that led down to Piper's Island restaurant, now dark and closed, and looked eastward. A few lights burned here and there in the flats that lined the Reading side; a car rumbled over Reading Bridge, visible ahead of us; and further off, a sudden stab of lightning illuminated brilliantly a mass of cloud towards London, turning it into a series of red, purple and pink blooms in the garden of the sky.

'Everywhere you look, there's always something beautiful, something miraculous,' said Taylor, half to himself.

'Define a miracle,' I replied, grinning.

'Being alive, for one,' he said. 'How you look at the world is another. If you go round gazing at your navel all the time, how can you possibly see how many stories, how many meanings, how much amazing shit there is in this world? You saw it tonight, with your little epiphany in the Turtle. Keep looking round, Dan; miracles happen everyday.'

'Yeah, but so does bad shit as well.'

'True, but whoever said a miracle has to be nice?'

'Oh balls, we're going to get drawn into an argument about semantics now aren't we? Let's not, eh? Let's just walk.'

Taylor laughed. 'As you want.'

So we strolled over the bridge and past the Crown and into Caversham. The odd car cruised past and the odd drunk tottered down the street.
'We all eventually have to make our way home somehow,' said Taylor, looking around.
'That sounds like something out of Reader's Digest.'
'Might be. I'm too tired to come up with original observations at this moment.'
'Does anyone ever come up with an original observation, though? Like you said earlier, everything we say's a copy of, or a comment on, everything else.'
'Did I say that? Someone must have said it first though, somewhere right over there, right at the beginning of it all.'
'I guess so.'
We turned the corner and went past the old telephone exchange, then crossed over again outside Tesco's. Passing the chemist and the restaurant, we saw a young man, no more than twenty, fast asleep on a bench. His arms were folded over his chest, and he was smiling faintly.
'Do you think he's happy?' I asked.
'He probably thinks he is,' Taylor replied. 'Whether he actually is, we'll never know. If you were in his body for a while, would you be happier than you are now or less? No way to know, man, no way to know. You can't measure feelings.'
'I wonder what he's dreaming?'
'Us,' said Taylor. 'We're his dream, and all this around him.'
'That'd piss off the Weirdo.'
'Too damn right.'
The library clock said that it was just past three. The figure of Old Father Time upheld it on his shoulders, and with one limestone hand was looking down over St. Martin's precinct and southwards.
'Looks like he's waiting for the dawn,' said Taylor. 'I suspect we'll be doing the same.'
We turned down Hemdean Road, past silent, dark houses. Although the air was fresher than before, it was still a warm, gentle night, pervaded with the scents of different nocturnal flowers. We came by the doctor's surgery and the path that led up to Balmore Hill.

'Let's go up here,' I said. 'We'll sit at the top, watch the town and wait for it to start getting light.'
We climbed the steps and found the bench at the top, which was reasonably clean. Someone must have had the same idea as us, because we could just make out a silhouette in the grass to our left as we sat down. Beneath us, Caversham lay flat, discernible as only a collection of roofs and streetlights. Beyond the river, marked only by a line of dark trees waving gently, was Reading, a constellation of lights, a jumble of office blocks. The gas towers at the mouth of the Kennet were large dark squares; the spires of St Giles, Christchurch, and St Lukes balanced stars and clouds on their tips; and there was the gentle rumble of traffic on distant roads, punctured by the insistent wail of a police car or ambulance now and then. Above us, there no planes flew by, although it would only be a couple of hours before aircraft began stacking in the sky to land at Gatwick or Heathrow, or begin the weary flights across the Atlantic to America. Far off to the south, probably above Whitley, a helicopter droned, and a light stabbed downwards from it – the police chopper in action. Up here, though, all was silence and relaxed. Taylor cracked open his can of coke, took a sip, and passed it to me.
'Cheers.' I took a sip, then another when I realised that I was far thirstier than I'd thought. I pulled my pack of cigarettes from my rear pocket, and extracted two battered and bent fags. I passed one to Taylor and we sparked up.
'You got any more?'
'No. Not that I really feel like another one, anyway. Nice up here.'
'Yeah, it's not bad. Nice view of the town. During the Civil war, the parliamentarians and the royalists fought up here, apparently. Then there was a load of hand-to-hand fighting. The corpses were buried where they fell, right under our feet.'
'Thanks for sharing that with me. Where'd you hear that?'
'Read it somewhere. Probably in the museum when I was a kid.'
A train rumbled and clattered along the railway, beginning to our left and passing through the town until it disappeared west and north, following the line of the river.
'That sound's nostalgic,' I said, referring to the train. 'You can hear the trains all the way round the valley on a still night. You

can even make out the announcements at the station. When I was a kid, I'd listen to this clunk and rumble as they went over the points, and imagine it wasn't a train I could hear, but a helicopter flying lazily overhead. I imagined that the helicopter was there to protect me from whatever the night could throw at me.'

'Looks like that came true,' murmured Taylor, waving the coke can at the police chopper, which was now flying off towards the west.

'Are you happy to be back here, Taylor?'

'Back in the UK, you mean? I'm content wherever I am. You know me, Dan. I don't feel the need to settle down, or anything like that. I don't need much. I don't have many ties. What about you?'

'Happier for seeing you, man, happier for seeing you.'

'Thank you,' and he smiled in the darkness. He was silent for a couple of minutes, then turned to me and said, 'so when *are* you going to contact Beattie?'

'Tomorrow. Or the day after, depending on when I wake up.'

'Do it tomorrow.'

'OK, Taylor.'

And we sat on the bench and watched the night creep past, often in silence, sometimes in chat. We lapsed into nostalgia, and talked about the places we'd gone and what we'd seen; we reminded each other of things the other had forgotten, or shed light on memories that had become silent and dark in our minds. We took a remembered and re-imagined journey from India to Britain, and in the maps that existed in our minds we filled in the blank spaces left after we'd parted company. Gradually, the sky lightened to the east and the day began to blossom. The noises of a wakening Saturday began; someone coughing, a dog barking, the drone of a milkman's float. We got up then, stretching our legs and feeling our stiff backs, and walked up the hill, up to Emmer Green and my digs, and sleep took us just as daylight began in earnest.

An Email

Hi Beattie!

I'll bet you're surprised to hear from me. It's been a long time, hasn't it? I've just seen Taylor, and he said he'd seen you in Bangkok, and he made me realise how longs it's been since we talked. How are you? What are you up to? I'm fine – stuck in grotty old Britain. I'm working in this office, but I don't think I'm going to for much longer.

Beattie, it's taken me an hour and a half just to write this far, and now I'm going to say all this in a rush, because if I don't I never will, if you see what I mean. You know what us Brits are like – we find it hard to say stuff. You and I never got together, though I don't know why. Well, yes I do actually – we were too bloody shy. The fact of the matter is that I like you a hell of a lot, and going out with Taylor for a drink or two (!) made me realise exactly how much. I want to be with you, Beattie. The thing is, do you want the same? I was so afraid of writing to you, because I was so scared of a reply that I wouldn't like; then again, how could you reply if I hadn't written a damn thing?

I know I'm making a mess of this, but what do you say? Do you want to make a go of things with me?

All my love,
Dan.

A Note.

And that's where the story ends. I thought long and hard about whether to include the email as a sort of coda, but Beattie said that it made sense. I don't argue much with her on that kind of thing, as she has a greater sense of acuity. I know that it's not the most exciting story in the world, but it's my story. Taylor was right about one thing, though – the Weirdo's notes were very interesting, and very useful for putting this all together. I have tried to recall everything as it happened, and I believe I've managed to get all that we said and talked about as accurate as possible. It's entirely likely that I've made errors, however; after all, who has a perfect memory, especially after such a time? I've conveyed the feeling, at least.

What I find somewhat amusing, and of course ironic, is that instead of the Fucking Weirdo being my Creator, as he claimed, I've become his in a literary sense. As he said in one of his interludes, the most relevant of which I've included, he will be seen only as he is written here, rather than as an entirely rounded, 'real' being. Well, that's his own fault. I'm coming to the end of this now, and all that it remains for me to do is wind up this little commentary, edit the text and organise headings, chapters, summaries and quotes et cetera. I've used many of the quotes that the Weirdo had noted down, as they seemed to follow his criteria of relevance and irrelevance as he saw it. I've added a couple of my own, but I must say that I'm pretty useless at it; I just stole the quotes from other authors who'd used them to preface their works. They do kind of fit in, though, so it's Okay. Besides, doesn't everyone do it?

What amazed me as I put all this together though, is how much it wrote itself. It was as if the story wanted to be told. My only regret is that poor Taylor won't see it. This was the last time I ever saw him; let this be my memorial to him, a happy moment in life.

Beattie's calling me to lunch on the verandah, so I'm going to finish now. I wish you could be here – New England is so glorious in the autumn.. I leave this to you, then, and hope you enjoy it.
Dan.